Their Ragged Breaths Mingled. "There Could Be More Where That Came From...If You're Willing."

Cort's shoulder muscles tensed beneath her fingers. "Exactly what are you suggesting, Tracy Sullivan?"

She gathered her courage. "I'm not looking for a husband. You're not looking for a wife. But we're both adults with—" Heat prickled her skin "—needs. We could um...explore those."

"Are you propositioning me?"

What if Cort turned her down? How would she face him for the rest of the summer? "I'm suggesting that perhaps we could fulfill those needs for each other."

He hesitated. "You sure about this? You wouldn't rather have some guy who could give you the ring, the white picket fence and the whole nine yards?"

"Yes."

Cort curled his long fingers around hers and lifted her hand to his mouth. His breath and then his lips whispered across her knuckles. "Then we have a deal. You'd better hold on to your shorts, Ms. Sullivan, because it's going to be a long, *hot* summer."

Dear Reader,

Welcome back to another passionate month at Silhouette Desire. A *Scandal Between the Sheets* is breaking out as Brenda Jackson pens the next tale in the scintillating DYNASTIES: THE DANFORTHS series. We all love the melodrama and mayhem that surrounds this Southern family—how about you?

The superb Beverly Barton stops by Silhouette Desire with an extra wonderful title in her bestselling series THE PROTECTORS. *Keeping Baby Secret* will keep *you* on the edge of your seat—and curl your toes all at the same time. What would you do if you had to change your name and your entire history? Sheri WhiteFeather tackles that compelling question when her heroine is forced to enter the witness protection program in *A Kept Woman*. Seems she was a kept woman of another sort, as well…so be sure to pick up this fabulous read if you want the juicy details.

Kristi Gold has written the final, fabulous installment of THE TEXAS CATTLEMAN'S CLUB: THE STOLEN BABY series with *Fit for a Sheikh*. (But don't worry, we promise those sexy cattlemen with be back.) And rounding out the month are two wonderful stories filled with an extra dose of passion: Linda Conrad's dramatic *Slow Dancing With A Texan* and Emilie Rose's supercharged *A Passionate Proposal*.

Enjoy all we have to offer this month—and every month—at Silhouette Desire.

Melissa Jeglinski

Melissa Jeglinski
Senior Editor, Silhouette Desire

Please address questions and book requests to:
Silhouette Reader Service
U.S.: 3010 Walden Ave., P.O. Box 1325, Buffalo, NY 14269
Canadian: P.O. Box 609, Fort Erie, Ont. L2A 5X3

EMILIE ROSE

A Passionate Proposal

AJ's Books & Java
Basha's Plaza
300 W. Apache Trail #120
Apache Junction, AZ 85220
480-288-0369

O O O O O O O O O O O O

▼ Silhouette®

Desire

Published by Silhouette Books
America's Publisher of Contemporary Romance

Pattie, thanks for pitching them over the plate.
Candy, Kim and Sally, you gals make this business
more fun than it ought to be.
And to Diane, thanks for the insight into your job.

 SILHOUETTE BOOKS

ISBN 0-373-76578-9

A PASSIONATE PROPOSAL

Copyright © 2004 by Emilie Rose Cunningham

This edition published by arrangement with Harlequin Books S.A.

® and TM are trademarks of Harlequin Books S.A., used under license. Trademarks indicated with ® are registered in the United States Patent and Trademark Office, the Canadian Trade Marks Office and in other countries.

Visit Silhouette at www.eHarlequin.com

Printed in U.S.A.

Books by Emilie Rose

Silhouette Desire

Expecting Brand's Baby #1463
The Cowboy's Baby Bargain #1511
The Cowboy's Million-Dollar Secret #1542
A Passionate Proposal #1578

EMILIE ROSE

lives in North Carolina with her college-sweetheart husband and four sons. This bestselling author's love for romance novels developed when she was twelve years old and her mother hid them under sofa cushions each time Emilie entered the room. Emilie grew up riding and showing horses. She's a devoted baseball mom during the season and can usually be found in the bleachers watching one of her sons play. Her hobbies include quilting, cooking (especially cheesecake) and anything cowboy. Her favorite TV shows include Discovery Channel's medical programs, *ER, CSI* and *Boston Public*. Emilie's a country music fan because there's an entire book in nearly every song.

Emilie loves to hear from her readers and can be reached at P.O. Box 20145, Raleigh, NC 27619 or at www.EmilieRose.com.

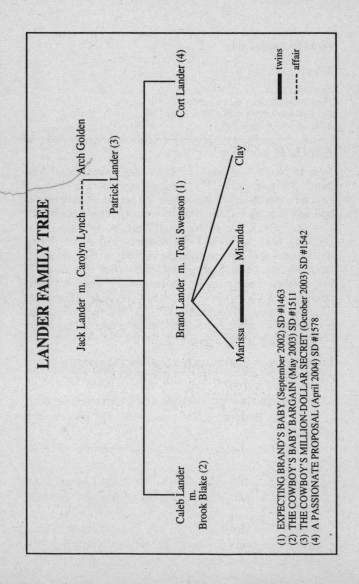

LANDER FAMILY TREE

Jack Lander m. Carolyn Lynch - - - - - Arch Golden

Caleb Lander
m.
Brook Blake (2)

Patrick Lander (3)

Brand Lander m. Toni Swenson (1)

Cort Lander (4)

Marissa   Miranda   Clay

twins
- - - - affair

(1) EXPECTING BRAND'S BABY (September 2002) SD #1463
(2) THE COWBOY'S BABY BARGAIN (May 2003) SD #1511
(3) THE COWBOY'S MILLION-DOLLAR SECRET (October 2003) SD #1542
(4) A PASSIONATE PROPOSAL (April 2004) SD #1578

Prologue

Middle-of-the-night calls never brought good news.

Cort Lander smacked his cheek in an effort to wake himself and grabbed the phone before the second ring. "Hello?"

He squinted at the digital clock. Just because his last seventy-two-hour shift had only ended three hours ago didn't mean the hospital wouldn't call him to come back if one of his patients took a bad turn. He preferred it that way.

"Is this Cort Lander—former...companion of Kate Simms?"

A bitter taste filled his mouth. He hadn't heard from Kate in over a year. Who would be calling here for her? "Yes."

"I'm Helen McBride from Du Page County Social Services. I'm sorry to have to inform you that Ms. Simms was killed today."

His heart stuttered. He struggled with the tangled sheets and sat up.

"Kate's dead?" Bold and aggressive Kate. She'd vowed that nothing would stand in the way of her becoming the best criminal attorney to ever hit Chicago. He hadn't realized at the time that she'd considered *him* an obstacle. "How?"

"A client managed to get a gun into the courthouse. When the verdict didn't go his way, he—but that's not why I called, Mr. Lander."

"Doctor," he corrected automatically.

"I called to ask you to take custody of your son."

"My what?" Certain his sleep-deprived brain had misunderstood, he shoved a hand through his hair, shook his head to clear it and then turned on the bedside lamp.

"Joshua, your son."

"Kate and I didn't have any children."

"Before she passed away, Ms. Simms told us where to find you and asked us to make sure you came for the boy. You are his only living relative."

The hair on the back of his neck stood up. He had a son? Impossible, unless Kate had been pregnant when she left Durham to take the job in Chicago. She'd surprised him with a Dear John letter four months later, but she'd *never* mentioned a pregnancy. Hell, she hadn't even bothered to mention why she'd dumped him.

"I haven't seen Kate in—" he mentally counted back "—almost sixteen months. How old is the boy?"

"Nine months. I'm sorry. I know this is quite a shock, but you are named as the father on his birth certificate, and Ms. Simms listed you as Joshua's guardian in her will. You must come and get him."

"What's his blood type?" Blood wasn't conclusive,

but he knew Kate's was O negative because she'd donated frequently. His was AB positive.

He heard the crackle of shifting papers over the phone line. "Josh's blood type is AB positive."

His gut clenched and his heart pounded harder. His palms started to sweat. The phone nearly slipped from his fingers. The calm he prided himself on when dealing with patients in the hospital vanished.

"I'm not taking custody until a DNA test proves he's my son."

"I certainly understand how you feel, Dr. Lander, but you are listed as the child's guardian regardless. You can certainly choose to give him up for adoption, but I'd suggest meeting Joshua first."

"Tell me where I can find him." He fumbled for a pen and paper and wrote down the address, and then he hung up the phone and put his head in his hands.

If Kate had had his baby, then why hadn't she told him? They'd parted on good terms—or so he'd thought until he'd received his walking papers. He'd planned to visit her during the holidays, but then she'd dumped him and refused to return his calls or his e-mails. Why? Had she found somebody new? Or had she finally figured out that a Texas cowboy would never meet her high expectations? She'd wanted blue blood, but he was blue collar.

He stood up and paced his bedroom, thankful that his roommates were all working the night shift, and he didn't have to explain the bombshell that had just dropped on his life. He wandered from room to room in the tiny two bedroom apartment he shared with three other medical residents.

What in the hell was he going to do with a baby? He couldn't bring him here.

He'd have to ask to be excused from the residency program early. Thank God summer break was only a few days away.

If the child was his he'd take him home to Crooked Creek. His brothers would know what to do with a baby. He'd call them and tell them... Oh, hell. He scraped a hand over his face.

He'd tell them the Lander curse had struck again.

One

The view from where he stood almost made Cort forget his brother had railroaded him into attending his high school's ten-year reunion.

A squeal drew his gaze from the rear view of the perfectly shaped female in front of him to the gal springing from her chair at the reception desk. She bounded around the table and hugged him. "Cort Lander. Oh my gosh. We had no idea you were coming. I thought you were in North Carolina."

The owner of those incredible legs stiffened in her sensible shoes but she didn't turn or interrupt her conversation with the man he recognized as his old gym teacher.

The squealer pointed to her puckered lips. "I'll forgive you for not letting me know you were coming if you plant one right here."

"I wouldn't do that if I were you," the woman with the great tush said as she turned.

Tracy Sullivan. He'd recognize her prim tone anywhere. A grin spread across his face.

Tracy's tightly twisted red hair had darkened to the color of the cinnamon sugar he sprinkled on his toast, but her serious caramel-colored eyes hadn't changed one bit. Neither had those lips. Damned if she didn't have the greatest mouth he'd ever seen, but as she'd been the sister of one of his teammates, that sexy mouth of hers had always been off-limits.

She moved forward. *Whoa,* where did she get those curves? Hadn't she been a beanpole in high school? His gaze rolled over hills and valleys he didn't remember, and his pulse accelerated.

Tracy's brows lowered in a mock scowl, but she couldn't completely suppress the smile twitching her lips. "Libby's married to the football coach, and if she doesn't stop accosting every man who comes through the door, her husband is going to tackle someone."

Libby ignored the warning, grabbed his shirt with both hands and yanked him forward. His gaze locked with Tracy's as Libby smacked her lips against the corner of his mouth. Libby turned him loose, grabbed Tracy's hand and dragged her forward. "Come on, girl, get yours."

His heart missed a beat. Normally he wouldn't let himself be coerced into kissing anyone, but the blush rising from Tracy's collar and spreading across the creamy skin of her cheeks was an endearing reminder of the freckle-faced girl who'd tutored him through high school English. Without her, he never would have graduated.

And it wasn't as if this was the first time he'd considered kissing her. He let his gaze drift to her lips, and his mouth dried.

Her blush intensified. "I don't think—"

He cupped his hand around her nape and smothered her protest with his lips. He meant to pull back after a quick buss, but his lips lingered on the softness of hers, sinking in and savoring. The sensation of coming home washed over him, which made no sense whatsoever since he and Josh had been home for days. Best he could figure it had something to do with her scent. Tracy smelled like home—hers, not his—apple pie and oatmeal cookies.

Her fingers curled into his chest, and her gasp of surprise pulled air from his lungs. His sanity followed right along behind it. Her silky hair brushed his knuckles, and his groin stirred.

A wolf whistle reminded him where he was and who he was with. *Tracy.* David's sister.

Down boy.

He released her slowly and struggled to regulate his breathing. His heart pounded in his ears like a jackhammer, and his blood raced through his veins as if pushed by a turbocharged engine. He hadn't been with a woman since Kate, and it was clear his body was aware of that fact.

That was the only reason kissing Tracy had set him on his ear. Wasn't it?

Tracy stood rooted to the spot, looking as stunned as she had the day she'd caught him skinny-dipping in Doc Finney's stretch of the Nueces River, and then she gathered herself and went starchy—the same as she had a decade ago. She might be aiming for cool, but the rapid rise and fall of her breasts beneath her blue dress told another story. "That was unnecessary."

Unnecessary and probably unwise, but he couldn't help wanting to kiss her damp lips again. He grinned and shook his head at the absurdity of wanting to kiss his pal, his buddy, his drill sergeant. "Time looks real good on you, Trace."

Her face took on a tomato hue, and her fingers knotted. "I…you…thank you, Cort."

They stood there gawking at each other until Libby grabbed each of them by the elbow and steered them toward the darkened corner of the gym reserved for dancing. Cort nodded to old acquaintances as they passed, but Libby's frog march didn't allow him time to stop and talk.

"Isn't Cort just the hunkiest thing, Tracy? Y'all dance and I'll cut in when my shift at the welcome table is over." Libby left them.

He faced Tracy and extended his hand. Her gaze bounced off his and returned. After what looked like a bracing breath, she curled her fingers around his palm. A hot flush washed over his body just as it had the first time he'd taken Tracy into his arms. He tried to concentrate on the up-tempo country song, but he hadn't two-stepped in years. His movements were awkward and the distracting reaction of his body to Tracy's wasn't helping his coordination, since the oxygenated blood from his brain pooled about a yard short of his feet.

They'd only taken a dozen steps when Tracy scolded him. "You shouldn't let Libby's silly challenges goad you into action. I swear, you'd think people would change in ten years, but—"

"It's good to see you, too," he interrupted. Chuckling, he shifted his hand on her waist, searching for a spot where the heat of her skin didn't penetrate the thin fabric of her dress to singe his palm.

"I didn't know you were home." Did he imagine the hitch in her voice?

"I've only been here a few days, and I won't be staying long." As soon as he figured out how in the hell to put his life back together, he'd return to Durham.

"You're still in the residency program at Duke?"

"Yes, I...took some time off." Tracy had always expected the best from him, and for some reason he didn't want to admit to her that he'd been hit by the Lander curse. He'd screwed up and gotten a woman pregnant the same way his father and one of his brothers had. A medical school graduate ought to know better.

Twenty-one pounds of hindsight had dropped in his lap last week, and he still hadn't figured out how he was going to handle that much...*knowledge* and continue his training.

The band switched to a slow ballad, and the lights dimmed. He pulled Tracy closer, but she stiffened and leaned away. "We don't have to do this."

"Why not? It's not like we haven't danced before. Prom night. Right here in this gym. Remember?"

And just like prom night, he couldn't control the action going on in his britches. Come on, man, get a grip. This is your pal, Tracy.

Her lush lips flattened. "I remember."

Whoa. Definite frostbite. Either she'd guessed his struggle or... "Do I have bad breath or something?"

She glanced at his mouth and then away. His lips tingled. "No, but I'd rather not take a trip down memory lane."

"Isn't that what a reunion is all about?" She squirmed in his hold, looking ready to bolt. Reluctant to let her go, he changed the subject. "What are you doing now?"

"Teaching."

Surprise made him stumble or maybe it was exhaustion. His thigh brushed between hers, and a distracting prickle followed his veins uphill. Oh man. Another jolt like that and everybody in the gym would be able to see his adolescent reaction. "I didn't know you wanted to teach."

"We never discussed my plans. We focused on your goals." Her gaze never left his chin.

"Ouch. Was I a selfish SOB?"

"No. You were the youngest in your family. The world tends to revolve around the one occupying that niche." He didn't hear a reprimand in her tone, only a statement of fact.

It was his turn to squirm. "And you were the oldest, the one in charge of the Sullivan herd. Are you still cracking the whip over David and the rest of your brothers and sisters?"

Her gaze flicked to his and away again before he could figure out what kind of thoughts she had running around in her head. "My family's still around."

No doubt her siblings had left her holding down the fort with the parents—not that she'd complain. Tracy had always been big on responsibility. "Where are you teaching?"

"Here."

"Here, as in Texas or here as in…here?"

"I teach English *here* at County." Her expression dared him to make something of it, and her spine stiffened beneath his fingers. He fought the urge to massage the tense muscles.

"You're probably good at it, but I'll bet you're

tough. You were with me, and I can't tell you how much I learned to appreciate that once I hit college.''

His comment seemed to fluster her. ''Yes, well, I'm hoping to become the principal soon—if I can penetrate the all-boys club.'' Pride and steely determination tilted her chin and exposed the slim column of her neck bared by the V-neck dress.

He struggled with an unexpected impulse to bury his face in the pale skin and cleared his throat. ''So you're doing well?''

She focused on a point beyond his shoulder. ''Yes, my career—my life—is right on target.''

Good. At least somebody's was. His sure had taken an unexpected detour, and where he'd go from here was anybody's guess. He had to figure that out—pronto.

An enthusiastic couple careened in their direction. Cort shifted his hold and swung her out of the way. His feet tangled as if someone had tied his shoestrings together, and he ended up pressed against Tracy from shoulder to knee. She went poker stiff, and he realized he had a handful of the curvaceous bottom he'd admired earlier. Dormant hormones awoke with the clamor of a marching band and paraded south in formation. Swift and unexpected desire made his mouth water and his skin flush.

For Tracy. Oh, hell.

His weird thoughts had to be a by-product of exhaustion. He hadn't had a good night's sleep since he'd picked up Josh. The kid cried all the time and his sleep cycle was nonexistent. They'd both be happier as soon as he could figure out why.

''Excuse me.'' The chill in her voice and the look in her eyes warned him he might lose a few digits—among other things—if he didn't move. Fast.

He missed another step and slid against her. The hard tips of her soft breasts teased his chest. His senses rioted. She couldn't possibly miss his condition. Embarrassed, he put a few inches between them.

"Do you mind if we sit the rest of this one out? I could use some caffeine." Or a cold shower.

"By all means. Refreshments are this way." Was that a quaver in her voice? Tracy pulled free and led the way across the gym in a long, sure stride.

For several seconds his knees locked, refusing to move. When did she add that seductive sway to her walk? He gave himself a mental kick in the pants and followed at a slower pace. His professor of abnormal psychology would have a field day with this. Was the combination of fatigue and sex deprivation the root of his problem? Or had bookworm Tracy Sullivan transformed into a goddess sometime during the past decade?

He shrugged it off. Either way it didn't matter. He wouldn't be here long enough to find out. Besides, even if he didn't have to worry about her brother anymore there were some things a guy just didn't do with a pal. Loving 'em and leaving 'em ranked number one on the list.

She handed him a glass of soda when he reached her side, and he chugged the icy liquid.

Libby bounced up. "Hey, you two, this isn't a funeral."

He welcomed the interruption and tried to realign his thinking while Libby babbled at an auctioneer's pace about who'd done what, when and where. Cort lost track of her convoluted tale, focusing instead on the emotions chasing across Tracy's face. Had he offended her?

His brain tuned back in when Libby said, "Tracy is without her usual summer nanny job and without a tenant for her upstairs apartment. And if I know you, Tracy, you've spent every spare dime on your baby brother and your needs-to-get-a-life-and-a-job sister. What will you do for money?"

Tracy looked mortified. "I will manage."

"Didn't you just pay Vance's tuition for next semester?"

Could Tracy's youngest brother be old enough for college?

"Libby—"

"I swear your family wrings every last cent out of you."

"Enough, Libby."

Whoa. That must be the voice she would use to yank students back in line. It sure made him stand up straighter. He wiped a smile off his face, remembering the times in her momma's kitchen when she'd used that tone to haul him back on task. Yes, now that he thought about it, he could see her as a teacher. She'd always maintained order in the chaos of the Sullivan kitchen.

"I'm certain Cort would rather talk about his training. What are you studying now, Cort?" She stretched her lips into a smile that didn't reach her eyes.

He winked to acknowledge her change of subject and almost forgot her question when she bit her lip and flushed. "I just finished my E.R. rotation. I'm specializing in cardiothoracic surgery."

"Oooh, *E.R.*," Libby gushed. "I love that show."

Tracy's smile faded and a frown pleated her brows. "What happened to your plan to come back here and practice at Doc's clinic?"

"Dad."

She laid a hand on his forearm. "You chose cardio because of your father's heart attack?"

Tracy had always been a toucher, but he didn't remember her touch burning his skin before. He shoved his hands in his pockets. "Without that surgeon, Dad wouldn't have made it."

She snatched her hand away and knotted her fingers. "Your father seems very happy with Penny. Married life suits him."

"Yes, it does." Cort hadn't been home five minutes before he figured out that he was a lone wolf—albeit with a cub in tow. His father had remarried, and each of his brothers had wives and children. Crooked Creek, the family ranch where he'd grown up, now belonged to his older brother Patrick.

He felt like an intruder at the ranch, but he had no idea where else to go or what to do with himself and his son for the summer. Taking Josh back to the two-bedroom apartment he shared with three other medical residents was out of the question, because even if he could find child care, his roommates wouldn't tolerate a baby crying in the middle of the night.

He couldn't keep imposing on Patrick and his wife, Leanna, but he'd yet to come up with an affordable alternative. "What's this about being a nanny? I would think you'd have had enough baby-sitting when you were younger."

"I did, but working for this family each summer gives me an opportunity to travel. We toured Europe last year and the Hawaiian islands the year before that. We were headed for Australia this year."

"Sounds fun." He didn't remember Tracy ever doing anything just for the hell of it. He'd tried and failed to tempt her into playing hooky numerous times.

"Enjoyable and educational," she corrected.

That was Tracy. To her, both words meant the same thing. He bit down on a smile. If he'd ever figured out a way to convince her that skipping homework could be educational, he might have stood a chance at getting her to cut loose.

Beside him Libby wiggled to the music. "Are you married, Cort?"

"No." And with Josh in the picture, he wouldn't even be dating anytime soon, but he wasn't about to tell Libby about Kate or the surprise she'd left him. It'd be all over town before sunup.

Libby gaped. "Why not?"

Tracy pinned him with a look that made him feel as if he'd forgotten his homework. "My training comes first and I still have five years to go."

Libby shimmied. "But aren't you already a doctor?"

"Yes, but I'm not a surgeon."

"Oh, please, a doctor's a doctor. I want my dance." Libby grabbed his elbow and dragged him toward the dance floor.

Tracy released her breath and touched her fingertips to her lips. Running into Cort Lander was *not* the highlight of her evening.

She'd been over her crush on him for years. Hadn't she? So why had her body flushed the minute she'd heard Libby say his name? And why did her thoughts scatter like dandelion seeds on the wind each time he touched her? And that kiss! She'd nearly collapsed at his feet. Her knees might never recover.

She tried to look away from the couple on the dance floor, but couldn't. Cort had changed. He'd left home as a rough-and-ready cowboy, but he'd returned with an urban polish. His thick, dark hair smoothly cupped his head without a single glossy curl out of place. Time had chiseled away the youthful softness of his jaw, deepened his voice and erased every hint of the slow Texas drawl that used to make her melt like ice cream in July. Unfortunately, the changes had only improved on an already potent product.

She couldn't remember ever seeing him in anything other than jeans or a basketball uniform. Tonight he seemed taller in his pressed khakis, and his shoulders looked broader beneath a pale yellow oxford cloth shirt. The man oozed confidence, and darned if she didn't find that incredibly sexy.

Good Lord, would she never learn?

She shook her head and sipped her cola. Remember what had happened the last time you gave your heart to Cort Lander? When he'd asked her to the senior prom, she'd thought he returned her feelings. Instead, he'd asked her because her brother had told him that no one else had. A pity date.

She had his basketball buddies—her brother among them—to thank for clearing up that little misconception.

Her only consolation was that Cort apparently never had a clue about the colossal crush she'd had on him in high school.

On the positive side, if bad things came in threes, then between her tenant bailing, her summer job fizzling and the man of her adolescent dreams reappearing she'd met her quota this week. Her luck should now take a turn for the better.

Cort looked up and his gaze met hers across the crowded gym floor. The corner of his mouth tilted in a sympathetic smile, and something inside her twisted. What was Libby telling him now? She cringed. Her best friend was well acquainted with every dirty secret Tracy owned, and bless Libby's heart, if she knew something, then everyone else soon would. She hadn't earned the nickname of Loose Lips Libby for nothing.

She could imagine the words "Tracy must be the oldest virgin in McMullen County. Can you believe it? And since she hasn't had a date in the last five years her status isn't likely to change."

Libby told her often enough to get out there and play ball so that she'd be familiar with the rules of the game. Unfortunately, Tracy had known the entire male population of the area since kindergarten and didn't have the slightest urge to become intimate with any of them. Her lack of interest probably had something to do with the knowledge that most of them were proud of their ability to burp the alphabet.

Swallowing hard, she smoothed her hands over her new linen dress. She'd have to cut in before Libby blabbed more secrets, and that held about as much appeal as a root canal.

Calm. In control. Professional. Silently reciting her mantra, she inhaled and exhaled. She could do this, but it would have been easier if Cort had widened around the middle and thinned on the top like most of their classmates.

It would be easier if she didn't still feel the imprint of his hand on her butt.

At that moment Cort yawned and stumbled again. The man must be exhausted. Honestly, some people had no sense of when to quit partying and go home to bed.

Tsking, Tracy marched across the floor and tapped her friend's shoulder. After a sly look, Libby surprisingly relinquished her prize without argument.

This time Tracy ignored her embarrassment and looked at Cort—*really* looked at him—noting the purple smudges beneath his brown eyes and the tired slump of his wide shoulders. She fought the urge to smooth his dark hair and pull his tired head to her shoulder. Her heart quickened just thinking about such a bold move, but of course she'd never do such a thing—especially with so many people watching.

"You're dead on your feet. Why are you here when you should be in bed?" She hoped he didn't notice the catch in her voice when his fingers curled around hers or the fact that she had never learned to dance worth beans.

Cort's brows rose, and a teasing sparkle lit his eyes. His amazingly sensual mouth curved in a smile. "Is that an invitation?"

Her cheeks flamed and her stomach dropped to her shoes. She glanced over her shoulders to make sure no one had overheard. "It most certainly is not. With the way you're stumbling around, you're an accident waiting to happen."

"And I thought you liked my style." He tried and failed to smother another yawn as he two-stepped her around the floor.

She didn't take it personally—even though one of her dates in college had informed her that she could bore a man to death. "Your style is absent tonight...along with your coordination. Would you like for me to drive you home?"

"I can make it under my own steam."

He looked as if he'd doze off standing up if he stopped moving. "Twenty miles down a straight, dark stretch of road? I'm afraid you'll fall asleep at the wheel."

"Are you trying to mother me, Trace?" A gentle smile touched his lips.

She winced. According to her siblings, she mothered everyone. "No. Yes. Probably."

"Thanks. I'll accept your offer." He yawned again. "Guess I'm not much of a party animal tonight, but I sure am glad I came. Wouldn't have wanted to miss seeing you."

Warmth swept through her, but she stopped it. Cort was just being polite. He'd always been polite. Too polite. Back in high school she'd wished just once he would grab her and kiss her senseless. She'd have willingly done whatever he wanted in the back of his pickup, but he'd saved that treat for the more popular girls. That was then, and now she had better sense. Thanks to her youngest sister, she'd learned exactly what folks around here called gals who did such a thing.

"My car is the dark-blue sedan parked near the flagpole. I'll meet you there in five minutes."

His brows dipped. "We can't leave together?"

"People will talk."

"If you don't want to be seen leaving with me, then I'll get myself home."

God save her from the male ego. Oh, bother. "Let me tell Libby where I'm going and why."

Five minutes later Cort crammed his long-legged frame into the passenger seat beside her. The car seemed darker, smaller and more intimate than when she'd parked it two hours ago. Lord, the man smelled good—like one of those expensive samples that came in her magazines. She tried not to be obvious when she drew in another whiff and then exhaled shakily.

"In a few minutes you'll be home and tucked in."

He slanted a sexy, sleepy look in her direction, and she nearly backed into the flagpole. Her mouth dried and her heart hammered. She double-checked to make sure her fingers hadn't turned into thumbs on the steering wheel, because it certainly felt that way.

A mile down the road the tightness in her throat subsided enough for her to ask, "Are you and your brothers keeping late hours catching up?"

Silence. Tracy glanced at Cort as she drove beneath the area light at the Farm and Ranch Store. He'd fallen asleep. The straight road and the full moon gave her the opportunity to look her fill. Once she'd dreamed of marrying this guy and living happily ever after. But, of course, that was before she'd discovered his plan to go to college halfway across the country. Just as well, popular jocks like Cort never dated geeks like her except out of pity.

Minutes later she parked in front of the Lander home. Moonlight slanted through the windshield, and a cool breeze swept fresh air through the open car windows. Being with Cort brought back bittersweet memories, which she'd deliberately suppressed in the past few years. She didn't like remembering where she'd come from. Instead, she focused on where she was going.

Their community didn't have a train track, but it did have a landfill, and the Sullivan house was on the wrong side of it. Folks had pitied them, donated clothes and old toys to them, but she'd never noticed Cort looking down his nose at her. He never seemed to see the shabby house and furnishings, and he never complained about her siblings storming through the kitchen for snacks during their study sessions. If anything, he seemed to like coming to her house for tutoring. As long as the cookie jar was full, Cort had been a willing visitor.

Much as she would like to sit here and reminisce, she had to get back to the gym before folks—namely

Libby—started talking. Curving her fingers over the thick muscles of his shoulder, she shook him awake. "Cort, you're home."

His eyelids slowly lifted and he smiled sleepily. "Thanks, Trace. You're a pal."

"So I've been told. Good night, Cort. I'll see you around."

He leaned over and brushed his lips against hers before she realized his intentions. Her heart pounded, and she had to fight the urge to twine her arms around his neck. She'd come a long way in the past decade, but men like Cort never settled for less than the best. He sat back and she licked her lips. His taste lingered.

"Count on it." He winked and sauntered away.

Two

Cort eased into the house as quietly as possible, pausing to listen for Josh's wail. Silence, blessed, rare silence greeted him.

He leaned against the door and wiped a hand over his mouth. He'd kissed Tracy—twice—and wanted to again. Was he nuts?

Stepping into the den, he flipped the light on—oh, hell—and flipped it back off when Leanna squealed, "Eeek!"

His brother was bare-assed and busy with his sister-in-law.

"Sorry." Embarrassed, he backed out of the room and hustled to the kitchen. A few minutes later his brother followed him in. Cort said, "I'm sorry, man."

Patrick fixed himself a glass of water. "She'll get over it...eventually. You're home early. I didn't hear your truck."

"Tracy Sullivan gave me a ride. She was afraid I'd fall asleep at the wheel, probably with good reason. And I was worried about Josh."

"He went down about an hour ago. Fussy little critter, isn't he? He kept you up again most of last night?"

"Yeah. I guess that means he kept you up, too."

He shrugged. "Babies do that."

"Yours doesn't."

"Matt's two years old, and he didn't lose his mother and move halfway across the country in the last week."

"You think that's all it is? I know nothing about babies."

"Consider this a crash course. Besides, you have three brothers and six nieces and nephews who're willing to teach you everything they know. You'll get it…eventually."

"For Josh's sake, I hope you're right."

"Even though you didn't stay long, I hope the break tonight did you some good. You looked like you were about to lose it."

Cort shoved a hand through his hair. "I'm just not used to…"

"Struggling?" When Cort looked at him in surprise, Patrick continued. "You were the smart one who never had to work hard for anything. Struggling isn't something you've experienced."

His brother had no clue how hard he'd worked to get accepted into Duke and to get a partial scholarship. Cort owed Tracy for keeping his nose to the grindstone.

Patrick crossed to the bulletin board and pulled down a business card. "Do you remember Dr. Finney?"

"I ought to. He patched us up often enough, and I worried the tarnation out of him by following him around and asking him questions about his practice. My first paying job was mopping his clinic floors."

"I forgot about that. I know Josh is your first concern right now, but Doc Finney needs some help at the clinic. Here's his number."

In other words, big brother thought he needed to contribute to his bed and board. "I'm only here for the summer. Think he'd be interested?"

"Can't hurt to ask, and it'll further your training."

"I'll stop by the clinic tomorrow." He turned to leave the kitchen and stopped. "Patrick, if our being here is a problem…"

Patrick clapped a hand on his shoulder and steered him toward the stairs. "This is your home. It's not a problem, but make a little noise next time you come in."

She'd already had her three bad things this week. So why was Cort Lander standing on her front porch with a baby in his arms? And why, since she didn't really want to see him again, did her heart dance a jitterbug when his dark gaze swept over her?

Embarrassed to be caught in her ratty workout clothes, Tracy blotted the moisture from her forehead. She'd been exercising her behind off—literally. Her cheeks still burned when she thought about Cort grabbing a handful of her abundant derriere.

"Still have that apartment for rent?"

She took in the broad shoulders filling her doorway and the way his black suit accentuated his dark good looks and how his coffee-colored tie perfectly matched his eyes. Her mouth dried. In a word he looked scrumptious. It took her a second to process his question and form a coherent answer. "Yes, I still have a vacant apartment."

The baby's round face reddened as if he was winding up for a scream. His dark eyes filled with tears and his bottom lip quivered. Whose adorable baby was this and why had they left Cort in charge? He clearly had no idea what he was doing.

"Can we rent it?"

"We?" Her stomach dropped. He'd said he wasn't married, but did he have a significant other? If so, then why had he kissed her? She glanced over his shoulder, but no one waited in the cab of his truck.

"Josh and I. And I'd like to hire you to be his nanny for the summer."

Surprised, she looked at the baby again, this time noticing the similarities between the males on her porch. They shared the same dark hair, deep-brown eyes and straight nose, and although she'd never seen Cort pout, she'd bet his full bottom lip would look exactly the same if he poked it out that way. "Josh is yours?"

"Yes. Is the apartment furnished?" Cort jiggled the baby, but it seemed to agitate him more.

She couldn't explain the envy curdling in her stomach. Given that she'd practically raised her six siblings, she didn't plan to have children of her own—not that she had to worry about that since she couldn't get a date, let alone a husband. She certainly wasn't going to get upset just because some other woman had borne Cort's baby.

"Yes. Oh, give him to me. When did he eat last and oh…" The situation became clear as soon as her hand cupped his soggy bottom. "He needs a diaper change. Do you have a diaper bag?"

"It's in the truck." He looked reluctant to leave.

"Get it." On the way to the den she detoured by the linen closet to get a towel to lay Josh on. After spreading it on the rug, she put him down. "Poor fella. You're a mess, aren't you? And you're absolutely gorgeous."

Those big dark eyes studied her while she stripped off his terry cloth sleeper. "You look just like your daddy."

"Are you complimenting me or insulting him?" He set the diaper bag down beside her.

Her pulse raced. "You figure it out."

Josh reached for her, and Tracy couldn't help herself. She blew a raspberry on his bare chubby tummy. He cackled and windmilled his arms.

"How did you do that?" Cort looked stunned.

"What? Blow the raspberry?"

"No. You made him laugh. He only cries for me."

He wasn't kidding. The earnestness in his eyes tore at her heart. Did Cort have an ex-wife? A custody issue? For some reason that bothered her, and it shouldn't, because Cort's personal relationships were none of her business.

"Does his mother take care of him most of the time?"

"Kate's dead. I didn't even know Josh existed until last week. She didn't tell me she was pregnant."

She kept one hand on the squirming baby and pressed the other to the ache in her chest. Her eyes stung. "That's horrible. You weren't married?"

He hunkered down and dug a diaper and the wipes out of the bag. Their fingers brushed when she took them from him, and her heart skipped a beat. "No. We split up when she graduated from law school and took a job in Chicago."

"Why wouldn't she tell you about this beautiful little

boy?'' Tracy whipped off the soiled diaper, slipped on a fresh one and then tugged on a clean romper.

Cort crowded her, watching her as intently as if she were performing a delicate surgical procedure. Growing up in a small home with six siblings meant she didn't require much personal space, but she was very aware that Cort had invaded hers. It made her self-conscious to have him so close and watching her every move.

Besides, he looked and smelled divine, and after thirty minutes of aerobics she didn't.

''According to her neighbor, Kate didn't tell me because she didn't want me to give up my plan to become a surgeon. She knew that I'd been raised by my brothers while dad worked eighteen-hour days, and that there was no way in hell I would have repeated the absentee father scenario.''

''But to keep your son a secret...'' She reached out to offer comfort, but drew her hand back before making contact. Touching him last night had wreaked havoc on her senses.

''Don't feel sorry for me. Save your pity for him. He's stuck with a lame-ass father unless I—'' He stood and shoved his hands in his pockets.

''Unless you what?''

His jaw muscles clenched and he turned his head away. ''Nothing.''

''Cort?'' Slowly she rose to stand beside him. His gaze met hers, and she caught her breath at his tortured expression. ''You're not thinking about giving him up, are you?''

He shoved a hand through his hair and then massaged the back of his neck. ''I can't help wondering if he'd be better off with two parents or even one who won't be working the insane schedule of a surgical resident.

He's miserable with me. I don't even know when it's time to change his diaper.''

This time she didn't resist her impulse. She grabbed his biceps, tipped her head back and faced him eye to eye. ''I've never known you to fail at anything you really wanted to do. You'll learn how to be a daddy.''

''So I'm told.'' He didn't sound as though he believed it. ''If you agree to be his nanny for the summer, maybe you can teach me.''

His nanny. Seeing Cort every day. Having him live upstairs with his bed directly above hers. Oh, Lord. She laid a hand over the knot in her stomach. Could she do that without falling in love with him all over again? Could she survive him leaving her a second time and knowing this time he wouldn't be coming back?

She wet her lips and rubbed her temple. For sanity's sake she ought to refuse, but the doubts in his eyes made her want to pull him close. A remnant of common sense intervened. ''What about your family? Can't they help out?''

''My brothers think it's hilarious to watch me fumble around, because they claim they did the same thing. You'd never know it now. They're pros. My sisters-in-law are better, but all three of them are pregnant and battling morning sickness in addition to juggling their own kids and careers.''

''All three are pregnant?''

He shrugged. ''It's a planned thing. They're trying to have the babies close together.''

Josh smiled and blew spit bubbles, thoroughly enjoying his freedom on the floor. Cort knelt and gently, tentatively, smoothed his big hand over the baby's soft, dark hair. ''It's just me and the little guy. Poor kid. If anybody can teach me, Trace, it's you.''

Her heart melted.

Josh stiffened and whimpered.

Cort muttered under his breath and straightened. He reached in his coat pocket and extracted a slip of paper. "I had an interview at the clinic this morning. This is what Doc Finney is offering to pay me. I've made a list of my other expenses, but I don't know what you charge to nanny or for rent. Can we afford you?"

Tension squeezed her rib cage and her heart pounded in the confined space. Sharing her home with Cort would be opening herself to heartache all over again.

But how could she refuse? She gazed at his son. The child had just lost his mother. Could she contribute to him losing his father, as well? Her conscience would haunt her forever.

With his clean diaper firmly in place, Josh rolled over onto his belly and crawled across the floor. Tracy let him go. Her nieces and nephews visited often enough that she kept the house childproofed, and baby drool wouldn't show on her floral-patterned sofa.

Her hand trembled when she took the paper from Cort. Even after a decade his handwriting still looked familiar, and a lump formed in her throat. She studied the numbers and came to the conclusion that she'd have to manage on less money this summer, because she couldn't turn Cort and Josh away. Somebody had to teach Cort how to be a father before he made a mistake that she was sure he'd live to regret.

"Yes, you can afford me."

"Good. When can we move in?"

"Put away your money. I can pay my own deposit and first month's rent," Cort growled at his brother

Sunday afternoon in Tracy's upstairs apartment. His ears burned with humiliation.

"You have a kid to take care of, and now you're paying rent on two apartments. Let me help." Patrick had lowered his voice, but Cort was certain that Tracy, standing only a couple of yards away with Josh on her hip, could hear.

He peeled his gaze off the length of leg exposed by her shorts and glared at Patrick. "Dammit, I'm not one of your charities. I have three roommates sharing my other apartment, so you don't have to worry about my check bouncing and me moving back home."

"You didn't have to leave in the first place."

"Like hell, I—"

"Gentlemen," Tracy scolded in her teacher voice, and Cort jerked to attention. "Josh is getting sleepy. Could we save the bickering until after the crib is assembled?"

His pride took a kick in the kneecaps.

Patrick shrugged. "Sorry, Tracy, you know how it is to be the older sibling."

"Yes, I do, but perhaps you should remember that Cort is now twenty-eight, not eight. If he needs something from you I'm sure he's mature enough to ask for it." The understanding in her gaze washed over him before she glanced toward the numerous boxes stacked in the den and kitchenette.

She stepped closer and touched his shoulder. His skin ignited, and her cinnamon scent filled his senses when he inhaled. "Cort, could you find clean pajamas for Josh? I'll give him his bath while you two finish up."

"Sure." He searched a box until he found a pale-green one-piece thing. Tracy took it, and their fingers brushed. Damn, he needed sleep more than he thought if one touch could stimulate his heart into arrhythmia.

"Thanks," she said as she passed. He thought she sounded a little winded. Probably from bouncing Josh on her hip. For such a little guy, the kid was heavy.

His gaze slid from her white T-shirt over her departing rear and then down her legs. He didn't remember Tracy's legs—or any part of her for that matter—looking that good. He glanced up and caught his brother smirking at him.

Patrick turned for the door leading to the outside stairs and called over his shoulder, "I need to get the toolbox from the truck."

Cooing and splashing pulled Cort away from unpacking and led him to the bathroom. Tracy had Josh in the tub. The little tyke obviously liked Tracy bathing him. He didn't enjoy it half as much when Cort washed him. Smart kid. Tracy wasn't likely to let his slippery body squirm right out of her grip. He, on the other hand, thought the kid ought to come with handles and instructions.

"He loves the water," Tracy said without turning away from her charge. Josh splashed her and she squealed. After one startled moment, Josh chortled and slapped both hands into the water sending droplets everywhere.

The ache in Cort's heart intensified. He hadn't been able to coax a smile from his son, let alone make him laugh out loud.

Josh deserved better.

He grabbed a hand towel from the rack and stepped into the room to blot the moisture from Tracy's face. "I'd like it, too, if I had a pretty lady scrubbing my back."

A flush stained her pale neck and cheeks. "Aren't you supposed to be assembling the crib?"

"Patrick's getting the tools from the truck. I thought I might learn something in Bath 101." He lowered the toilet lid. It wasn't until after he sat down that he realized the room wasn't big enough for two—three if you counted the squirt. His knees bracketed Tracy, and his mind took an X-rated detour. Unless he wanted to embarrass himself, now was not the time to fantasize about Tracy on her knees in front of him.

He blew out a slow breath and focused on her hair. She'd tortured it into that tight twist again, and it looked like only one pin held it in place. The urge to pull the pin and see the strands tumble over her shoulders nearly overwhelmed him. He twisted the towel in his hands.

He'd liked her hair long, and so did Josh. His son's tiny fingers had played with the length of Tracy's braid yesterday while she changed his diaper. He wouldn't mind burying his own hands in the shiny strands to see if they were as soft as they looked.

He plucked at the collar of his knit shirt. The heat and humidity of the bathroom were getting to him. "You're good with kids, and it's clear you like them. Why don't you have a houseful of your own by now?"

"I spent my childhood mothering my brothers and sisters. It's time to put myself first. Kids aren't a part of my plan."

He wondered if his brothers had ever resented having to baby-sit him. Brand, Patrick and Caleb had been more like parents to him than his own father. He didn't remember his mother. She'd left when he was two.

Josh wouldn't remember his mother, either.

He shoved aside the sobering thought. "Do you put yourself first? From what Libby said, it sounds like you're still combining the roles of platoon commander and Mother Teresa.''

"Libby talks too much. Grab that towel and take this wiggly fella.'' She lifted Josh out of the water and turned.

The wet fabric of Tracy's shirt clung to the lacy bra and the peachy skin underneath, distracting him from the chore she'd assigned him. His abdomen tightened. He sucked a deep breath to clear his head. Tracy's sweet scent mingled with the baby bath soap to short-circuit a few of his brain cells.

"Cort?'' She sounded breathless.

He snatched up the towel and snapped it open. Tracy pushed Josh into his arms, and her fingertips grazed his chest. He flinched. The woman packed the electric charge of a defibrillator, and every time she touched him his heart took a jolt. He bundled Josh in the towel, terrified he'd drop him.

"Cort, relax. Your tension transfers to him.'' She kneaded his tense biceps, and other parts of his body tensed.

Sure enough, Josh's smile vanished and his lip quivered. Cort couldn't have been happier to hear Patrick's boots on the outside stairs. He passed Josh back to Tracy, and his knuckles inadvertently brushed her breast.

She gasped, and their gazes locked.

He hated the wariness in her caramel-colored eyes. He swallowed hard and shoved his hands into his pockets.

"Excuse me.''

Seducing Tracy was not part of his plan. He'd be in Texas less than three months, and Tracy deserved more than a quick roll in the hay. That was all he had to give.

Even if he were staying longer, he wasn't fool enough to offer another woman the opportunity to wipe her feet on his heart. "I'll call when his crib's ready."

He hustled out of the tiny bathroom. What was the matter with him? It had to be the sheer terror over being responsible for Josh, causing the tension in his gut and making his brow sweat.

He feared he would bungle being a single father as badly as his dad had—only Josh didn't have older brothers to pick up the slack.

Josh's crying woke Tracy at two in the morning.

She lay in the darkness waiting for the baby to settle, but he seemed to grow more agitated as time passed. Before going to bed tonight she and Cort had agreed on a tentative schedule. This was Cort's shift, but Josh had been crying for almost thirty minutes.

Throwing back the covers, she shrugged on her robe, climbed the inside stairs and knocked on the door. Cort didn't answer. He couldn't possibly sleep through the baby's crying, could he? She turned the knob and, finding the door unlocked, stepped into the apartment.

Cort, wearing nothing but scrub pants riding low on his narrow hips, paced the den with Josh crying on his shoulder. Muscles rippled in Cort's shoulders as he awkwardly patted and rubbed the baby's stiff back.

She could have lived without the knowledge that he had dimples flanking the base of his spine. Adrenaline coursed through her blood, erasing the remnants of sleep from her brain and turning her insides to mush.

"It's all right, kid. We'll get the hang of this soon. Everybody says so. Just put up with me until then, okay?"

Josh's piercing wail jerked her out of her hormonal

stupor. No wonder Cort hadn't heard her knocking. Before she could speak he reached the end of the room, turned and stopped in his tracks when he spotted her across his living room. "Damn. I'm sorry we woke you."

"You shouldn't swear in front of the baby," she corrected automatically.

Even in the dimly lit room she couldn't miss the well-defined muscles of his broad chest and shoulders. A small gold medallion glinted in the dark hair dusting his chest. Finer hair marked a path between his washboard abdominal muscles. She didn't want to consider what he was—or wasn't—wearing beneath the thin fabric of his scrubs. Cort had always been athletic, but ten years ago he'd been an eighteen-year-old boy. As a twenty-eight-year-old man, he'd matured beyond expectations.

Strange feelings stirred in her belly. She dampened her dry lips. "Did you change him and give him a bottle?"

"Yes to the diaper. No to the formula. The baby book says not to feed a nine-month-old more often than every six hours." He grimaced. "It also says to let him cry himself back to sleep, but I tried that, and I can't handle it."

His dark curls went every which way, reminding her that he'd also been in bed. She looked through the open door beyond his shoulder to the rumpled sheets on his bed, and her stomach clenched. "Sometimes it's best to ignore the books and go with your instincts. Would you like for me to fix his bottle?"

He shook his head. "Thanks, Trace, but if you think that's what he needs I'll take care of it. Leanna warned me to keep bottles already made in the fridge. You go back to bed."

If she had half a functioning brain she'd do as he suggested, but Cort and Josh obviously needed her. "Let me help."

She walked into the tiny kitchenette, opened the refrigerator and extracted a bottle. The cool air washed her hot cheeks. Lordy, the man exceeded every secret fantasy she'd ever dreamed up. Suddenly hot, she plucked at her robe.

While the formula heated in the bottle warmer she stepped closer to Cort and Josh and stroked a finger along the baby's damp cheek. "Hi, fella."

Josh whimpered and reached for her. After a second's hesitation, Cort passed him to her. Her forearm brushed his bare chest as she took the baby, and the skin on her arm burned as if she'd pressed it against the radiator in her classroom. The fine hairs on her body stood on end, and her toes curled in her slippers.

Josh immediately buried his face in her neck and clutched handfuls of her hair.

Cort gently extricated the tiny fingers and as he did so, his fingertips brushed the skin of her shoulders and neck. She hoped he didn't notice her goose bumps or the shiver she couldn't suppress. "He likes you better. Can't say I blame him."

Her heart clenched at the pain lacing his voice, and her pulse raced at his half-naked proximity. "He's probably accustomed to women taking care of him."

He parked his hands on his hips, and his muscles flexed in a most distracting way. The urge to smooth his rumpled hair, to test the suppleness of his skin or to trace the line of dark curls bisecting his navel was difficult to ignore. But ignore it she would.

When Cort turned away to get the bottle, she laid a hand over her misbehaving heart and took a moment to gather herself and her wayward thoughts. Calm. In control. Professional. You are his nanny now. Act like one.

A fragment of common sense asserted itself. "Shake the bottle well to avoid hot spots and test it on the inside of your wrist to make sure it won't burn his mouth."

He did and then offered her the bottle, but she shook her head. He had to learn. "Sit down. You give it to him."

Cort sat in the overstuffed chair, and Tracy placed Josh in his arms, being extra careful not to touch Cort's bare skin during the transfer. Cort nudged the nipple against Josh's lips, but the baby refused. "Come on, buddy. Fill your tank."

Josh wailed. Both males were as tense as a newly strung clothesline. She touched a hand to her temples and looked skyward. Why me? Is this some kind of test? She blew out a long, slow breath.

"Relax, Cort, or he won't either." Knowing she'd probably regret it, she stepped behind the chair and kneaded Cort's knotted shoulder muscles. The heat from his supple skin traveled from her fingertips to her breasts and thighs. Cort's tension ebbed from him to her, swirling in the pit of her stomach and coiling around her chest. She almost groaned aloud when she identified the cause. Desire.

Obviously, she'd never gotten over her crush on Cort Lander, except now she had the adult, X-rated version dancing through her mind and shortening her breath.

As Cort's muscles unwound, so did Josh's. After one last whimper, the baby hungrily latched on to the bottle.

Cort exhaled. "Can't say I blame you, kid. After the last hour I could use a drink myself."

Tracy dropped her hands to her sides, wiping them on her gown as if she could erase the feel of him from her memory. She had no need for inhibition-relaxing alcohol. Her senses were already spinning out of control.

She wanted the impossible. She wanted Cort Lander. "Don't forget to burp him."

She let herself out of the apartment before she did something foolish.

Who'd have expected practical, down-to-earth Tracy to have magical fingers or hair as soft as satin sheets?

Cort smothered a yawn and blinked his tired, gritty eyes. He'd kept an erection for hours after she'd left last night, and consequently, he'd hit the snooze button on his alarm clock one time too many this morning.

"Okay, kid, let's try this again." He tucked a spoonful of baby mush between Josh's lips. Josh promptly sprayed it all over him. Aw, hell. He'd have to change shirts, which meant he'd probably be late for his first day on the job.

"Can't say I blame you. This stuff looks and smells like casting plaster."

A tap on the inside door meant the cavalry had arrived. Remnants of last night's dreams jolted his libido and heart into overdrive. "Come in."

Tracy stepped over the threshold looking good enough to eat in jeans that hugged her hips and a peachy-colored top that reflected the blush on her freshly scrubbed cheeks. The thick braid of her cinnamon hair fell over her shoulder to loop around the tip of her breast like a lover's tongue. Oh, man. He clenched his teeth on a groan.

Tracy took one look at the situation and shook her head. "I have Cheerios downstairs."

Before he could say another word she vanished and

his heart sank, but she reappeared seconds later and deposited an armload of stuff on the table. He could have kissed her for coming back. He was definitely out of his element here, but he wasn't sure about the yellow box of cereal and the banana. "The book didn't say anything about regular food."

"Would you trust me on this one?" Her white teeth dug into her lush bottom lip, and he figured he'd probably agree to just about anything if she kept that up. Scraping a hand across his chin, he nodded. She had to know more about babies than he did, and he'd always been able to count on Tracy steering him in the right direction.

She set a bottle of stain remover on his side of the table and then scattered a few cereal rings on the high chair tray. Josh snatched them up, shoving them into his mouth as fast as a linebacker at a buffet. He greeted the banana with the same enthusiasm.

Tracy's gaze traveled over him. "You'd better change and get out of here."

"You're right. Thanks for helping." He stood and peeled off his shirt. Tracy inhaled swiftly. He hesitated. Did she feel the same fierce attraction that twisted his hormones into a pretzel? Or had he offended her? He started to shrug the shirt back on.

Her eyes were big and round and her cheeks bore a fresh wash of color. "It's okay. I've seen a man without his shirt before. I've seen *you* without your shirt before."

She'd seen him without more than his shirt that time she'd surprised him at the river. Did she remember? "So you have."

Her gaze drizzled over him like melting caramel. Did she have any idea what a look like that did to a man?

If he stood here long enough there'd be no doubt. He moved away from the table.

"Wait." Tracy moved forward and reached for him. Every muscle in his body locked. She picked bits of cereal from his hair, his ear, his eyebrow, and her featherlight touches nearly drove him out of his mind.

He clamped his lips closed and tried to breathe normally. Her scent filled his senses. She stood so close that all he had to do was lift his hands a few inches to span her waist. But he wouldn't. Casual friend-to-friend kisses and touches were one thing, but that wasn't what he wanted right now. Need charged through his body like a pack of hungry dogs. Need that would go unfulfilled. He clenched his fists.

Her gaze met his and her smile slowly faded. She lowered her hands, wet her lips and glanced back toward Josh. Her throat worked as she swallowed once, twice, and a dark flush swept her cheekbones. There was no mistaking the sexual tension clogging the air.

She cleared her throat and busied herself with cleaning up his breakfast dishes. "Tomorrow, I'll handle breakfast."

The last thing he wanted was to ruin their friendship.

"Thanks." His voice sounded as though he'd swallowed a handful of gravel. He beat a hasty retreat, eager, he was ashamed to admit, to get out of the house before he did something stupid like kiss her until they ended up naked and horizontal.

What he needed was a good dose of something that didn't make him feel like a failure. Work. He had an exemplary bedside manner, and his diagnostic skills were superb, or so his instructors back at Duke had told him.

Obviously, Josh didn't see the same qualities.

Cort shrugged on a clean shirt and tie. He'd never shirked hard work, but usually his diligence produced visible results. No such luck with Josh. The harder he tried, the worse the situation seemed to get with his son. The baby books were a prime example. He'd practically memorized the parenting books he'd found on Kate's shelves only to have Tracy tell him to ignore them and follow his gut instinct.

Not a chance. He trusted his gut when it came to patients, but not with his personal life, because with Josh and Tracy his gut was one big knot of apprehension.

Three

Tracy's heart quickened when Cort's truck pulled into the driveway that evening.

Libby had dropped by earlier to soak up all the news about Cort and Josh, and she'd stayed long enough to fill Tracy's mind with illicit suggestions regarding ways to convince her new tenant to stay in Texas. Seduce him, she'd said.

Tracy rolled her eyes. As if she'd know how to seduce anybody.

"Show him what he's giving up by going back to Duke. It's your last chance to hook the man of your dreams," Libby had insisted.

Tracy shook her head. She would never deliberately quash someone's dream. If Cort wanted to be a surgeon, then he ought to be a surgeon. He was her tenant. She was his nanny. She'd do best to remember that, but that didn't mean she didn't secretly wish she could be as bold as Libby suggested.

"Daddy's home, sport." Cort looked scrumptious in his dark suit and blinding-white shirt.

Josh took one look through the glass storm door at the man striding up the walk and buried his face in her neck. Cort witnessed the maneuver, and his confident stride faltered. Resignation settled over his features.

Tracy's heart went out to him. She vowed to do whatever she could to bring father and son together. Plastering a smile on her face, she pushed open the door. "How was your day?"

"Not bad." Satisfaction filled his voice. He lifted a hand toward Josh's back, but then dropped it before making contact. "How about here?"

"I think he'll be more comfortable once we unpack the boxes and find familiar toys."

"Probably." He inhaled deeply as if bracing himself for the worst and reached for Josh again. Josh's fingers tightened in the fabric of her top and he scuttled closer. Cort had never accepted failure well, and she could see that Josh's repeated rejections were beginning to wear him down. She had to do something before Cort quit trying.

"Why don't you slip into something more comfortable and come back downstairs?" She cringed when she realized her words sounded like bad dialog from a soap opera. Darn her fair, redheaded skin. She had to be crimson by now. "I've, um…started dinner."

With a twinkle in his eye and the lift of one brow, Cort let her comment pass. "I don't expect you to cook for me."

A wiser woman would limit the amount of time she spent with a man she'd futilely fantasized over for more than a decade, but until he got a handle on feeding Josh she didn't see that she had a choice. "You'll owe me a dinner."

He grinned. "Just like old times. I wouldn't be where I am today if it weren't for your tutoring. I owe you, Trace. You name it and if it's within my power, it's yours."

Libby's suggestions scrolled through her head and her blood simmered. "Yeah, and you stole valedictorian right out from under my nose for all my trouble."

"Your fault. You're too good a teacher." Cort turned back toward the front door, and Tracy hooked her hand through his elbow. He jerked to a stop and his muscles clenched beneath her fingers.

She withdrew her hand. "You might as well use the inside stairs."

He shrugged off his suit coat. "Aren't you worried about what the neighbors will say?"

It wasn't as if her family hadn't been the subject of gossip before, but the scandal had never been attached to *her*. "By now Libby's spread the news that you're my tenant and I'm your nanny."

With a nod he disappeared up the stairwell.

She shifted her gaze from his tight tush, which she had no business ogling, to the adorable baby in her arms. "You have to take it easy on him, sport. He's trying, and your daddy never settles for less than the best."

And she, unfortunately, had never been the best at anything.

Cort paused in the doorway of Tracy's kitchen. The homey atmosphere drained away the tensions of his day, and then his gaze fell on his son and his muscles knotted all over again.

Josh blew bubbles and babbled happily in his high chair. Tracy had won his son over in one day—something Cort hadn't been able to accomplish in a week.

Tracy, with her back to the door, stirred something on the stove that smelled good enough to tempt his taste buds, but her off-key humming and the swaying of her jeans-clad hips made his mouth water. Shaking his head, he tried to clear the inappropriate thoughts and concentrate on the hunger he could satisfy.

Josh's sudden silence alerted Tracy to his presence. She turned and a blush tinted her cheeks. "Grab the salads from the refrigerator and then have a seat and tell me about your first day at the clinic."

A grin tugged his mouth. She'd always been bossy, but for some reason Tracy's orders had never rankled the way his brothers' had. He did as she asked, settling in the chair closest to Josh and offering his son one of the graham crackers Tracy had left on the table. Josh hesitated and then took it and babbled something back. Progress.

Cort lifted his gaze from the boy to Tracy. "The clinic is different from what I'm used to. At the hospital we're trained to quickly and efficiently diagnose a problem and initiate a treatment protocol. Treat 'em and street 'em. Today my patients seemed more interested in prying personal information out of me than telling me their symptoms."

"Did you expect work to be the same in rural Texas as it is at a university hospital? The hospital teaches you to be detached. You focus on the illness. Here you're expected be a friend, a confidant. You'll not only treat the person, you'll be expected to know any extenuating circumstances that could have led to the problem. In other words, a country doctor is equal parts MD and psychologist.'' She ladled her concoction onto three plates.

''Doc says the same thing, but I won't be here long enough to get to know any of them that well.''

''They don't know that. To them you're a local boy who's done well and returned home.'' She set a plate in front of him and eased into a chair. Her movements were graceful and economical—a far cry from the awkward teenager he remembered. He didn't recall the generous curves beneath her T-shirt, either, but that was a path he didn't need to explore.

Chicken and dumplings had always been his favorite. Had Tracy remembered or was this just his lucky day? ''Libby's slowed down. No one asked me about Josh until lunchtime.''

Tracy grimaced. ''Every eligible female within an hour's drive will develop a health complaint over the next few days.''

He groaned. ''The last thing I need right now is to get tangled up with gals who dream of white picket fences. I'm not staying.''

Tracy bit her lip and poured him a glass of iced tea. ''You don't have to convince me. Think on the bright side. You'll probably see more naked single women in the next few weeks than any other man in the county does in a lifetime. My brothers will be jealous.''

He paused with his fork halfway to his mouth. ''Are you trying to kill my appetite?''

The teasing light in her steady gaze turned serious. ''Did you love Josh's mother?''

He nearly choked on the mouthful of delectable pastry. Swallowing, he considered his answer. ''I thought

I did. Kate and I dated for three years, and we'd discussed getting married after I finished my training.''

''Why wait?''

''Timing.''

She waited expectantly with her brows raised, as if there should have been more to his answer. He felt like a kid in class who'd been caught without his homework.

''A prominent firm in Chicago offered Kate a job too good to refuse, but I wanted to finish at Duke.''

''There are hospitals in Illinois and law firms in North Carolina. Either of you could have pursued your goals elsewhere.''

''Not with the kind of prestige she needed, and I wanted to study under Dr. Gibbons. He's supposed to be the best chest man in the country. In a few more semesters I'm hoping to be assigned to his rotation.''

She nodded. ''You refused to compromise. It's always been all or nothing for you.''

He shifted uncomfortably even though there wasn't any condemnation in her statement. ''I guess so.''

''If you really loved each other it seems like one of you would have been willing to make the sacrifice to stay together.''

He couldn't deny the thought had crossed his mind. Kate had turned down offers from prominent firms around Durham. She'd chosen her job over him and, sure, it rankled.

Had bad timing been the only reason he hadn't married Kate? Had she known before she left that she was going to dump him? If so, couldn't she have given him a clue? Or had she, and he'd been too wrapped up in his studies to see it?

Tracy fed Josh smaller bits of their dinner with far

more finesse than he'd managed thus far. "Tell me about Josh's mother."

Her request made his gut clench. He didn't want to talk about Kate. He hadn't gotten a handle on the anger he felt toward her for keeping her pregnancy a secret, but Tracy had given them a place to stay and she'd taken over Josh's care. He owed her. Again.

"Kate was determined to be the best criminal defense attorney in the world. She wanted to be the one called when the next high-profile case came along."

"And you admired that?"

"I respected her ambition. She knew where she wanted to go and had a plan to get there. There's something attractive about a woman who knows exactly what she wants and isn't afraid to go for it."

Tracy's hand stilled above her plate. Her gaze met his, and he could practically hear the wheels turning in her mind. Did she see the similarities between herself and Kate? "What about Kate's family?"

"She was an only child. Her folks died a few years back. I'm all Josh has."

She covered his hand with hers and his skin warmed. "He's a very lucky boy to have you and the Lander clan. Your brothers and sisters-in-law have become very involved with the community in the past few years. Brooke does her motivational workshop for the graduating seniors each year, and Patrick has started up a scholarship fund. You can be proud of your family, Cort. The Landers have come a long way from the dirt-poor days."

"A lot of good my family will do him when we're halfway across the country."

She pursed her lips and his focus shifted to her mouth. "That's certainly something for you to consider.

Are you seeing anyone now? Someone who might help you with Josh?''

"I'm seeing you." Seeing her in a whole new light. Tracy Sullivan had changed from a bookworm to a beautiful, confident woman while he'd been away. The irony of being sexually attracted to her didn't escape him. If anyone believed in families and forever, it was Tracy, but he liked her too much to sleep with her and then leave her to deal with the aftermath of an affair. It'd be the same as painting a scarlet *A* on her chest.

She pinned him with a schoolteacher stare. "That's quite amusing, Cort. Now answer the question."

"Even if I was interested in dating, the seventy-two-hour rotations would kill a relationship pretty fast. So, no, I'm not seeing anyone and have no plans to do so in the foreseeable future."

Somehow he'd have to find a way to become the father Josh needed, and the risk of failing this little boy scared him more than anything he'd ever faced.

"Cort." Tracy's voice and a soft touch on his arm jerked him awake.

It took him a second or two to realize he was in bed with Tracy beside him. He didn't know what she was doing there, but his wild dreams offered up a dozen hot suggestions. He discarded them when his blurred vision cleared, and he realized she was sitting on the edge of the mattress bundled in her bathrobe. "What's wrong? Josh?"

She stood, tucked her hair behind her ears and stuffed her hands into the pockets of her robe. "Doc Finney called. Sandra Addison is in labor. She's refusing to go to the hospital and insisting on a home birth. He wants your help."

His adrenaline kicked in. Swearing, he threw back the covers and heard Tracy inhale sharply. He didn't have time to be embarrassed over the visible result his steamy dreams had left under his scrub pants. "I'll call the phone company tomorrow and try to hurry them up about getting my line connected. I know middle-of-the-night calls weren't part of our deal, but can you watch Josh?"

"Of course. I'll sleep on the sofa so I can hear him."

He reached into the closet and grabbed pants and a clean shirt. "Not unless you know a good chiropractor. You can sleep in my bed. I don't have any communicable diseases."

Her gaze bounced from his to the king-size bed and back. Her hand covered her throat. "I...all right."

Stepping behind the door, he shucked his scrubs, pulled his pants over bare skin and shrugged on his shirt. His briefs were in the dresser across the room, but he had a feeling Tracy wouldn't appreciate him parading across the moonlit bedroom in the buff to get a pair—especially since he was still hard from dreaming about her. He took extra care zipping up.

"I'll get back as soon as I can." He stopped beside her and had to fight a strong urge to smooth her rumpled hair. The silky strands tumbled halfway down her back. Obviously, Doc Finney's call had yanked her out of bed.

Thinking about Tracy and bed wasn't something he needed to do if he wanted to walk without a hitch in his step. He patted her shoulder with an unsteady hand. "Thanks, Trace. I owe you."

Sunlight teased Tracy's eyelids. Warm and cozy, she burrowed farther under the covers until one cold, hard fact shocked her awake.

She'd spent the night in Cort's bed.

Shoving her hair off her face, she sat up and turned in the direction of Cort's low, rumbling voice. As if she'd conjured him up, he paced by the bedroom door carrying Josh and murmuring quietly. Her heart flopped like a fish on a dock.

Lordy, she must have slept like the dead after getting Josh down that last time. She hadn't heard Cort return. Where had he slept? Not on that awful sofa, she hoped. She made a mental note to throw out the back-breaking torture mechanism as soon as she could afford to replace it and turned her head. The pillow beside hers had a dent in it and a lone dark hair lay on the white case. She pressed a hand to her chest.

She'd slept with Cort Lander.

And nobody knew it. A thrill shot through her.

Libby's ridiculous suggestion to seduce Cort into staying popped into her head, and her pulse raced. No. No. No. It wasn't going to happen. A passionate fling was *not* on her agenda. No matter how tempting. No matter how many times she'd dreamed of having Cort as her first lover. He'd always been the unattainable jock—too good for her then and even further out of reach now.

She blew her hair off her face and rolled her eyes. Even if she had the power to make him want her she'd never be able to hold him.

But what would it be like to experience firsthand the intimate touch of a lover's hand? Cort's hands. A shiver worked itself through her body, peaking her nipples beneath her thin nightgown and giving her goose bumps. She scrubbed her hands up and down her arms.

Couldn't she guard her heart, if she knew going into

the affair that there would be no happily ever after for them?

No, it would be best if she focused on her goal of being the first female principal at County. She'd ceased being an object of pity when she'd earned her teaching certification, but she wouldn't be happy until she won the respect of those who'd once written her off as white trash.

"Morning." Cort stopped in the open door.

His sexy, morning-rough voice combined with her previous illicit thoughts caused her skin to tingle and her lower belly to ache. "Good morning."

He wore the same scrub pants he'd worn when she'd awakened him earlier—the same pants which had left *nothing* to the imagination about the impressive size of his arousal, which had thankfully subsided.

She swallowed the knot in her throat and tried to ignore the way his handsome, beard-stubbled face made her heart palpitate. "Have you been home long?"

The corner of his mouth tipped up, and mischief sparkled in his brown eyes. "You mean you slept through everything? I guess that means it wasn't good for you?"

Her skin caught fire. Cort had always been a tease. "I guess that means you're forgettable."

"Ouch. You used to be a morning person."

She still was…usually, but her hair probably looked like a rat's nest, and her gown was old and threadbare. Where had she left her robe? Through the door she spotted it hanging over the back of the couch. Lordy. Two thin pieces of cotton were all that separated them from nudists.

She struggled for sanity and tried to control her sudden shortness of breath. "Josh is teething. Some pediatric pain reliever might help. I'll buy a bottle today."

"He had a rough night?" He came closer, and she wanted to yell at him to stay away until she was back in her right mind.

"Yes. How's Sandra?"

He winced and disengaged Josh's fingers from his chest hair. "She and her new daughter are fine. I managed to convince them to go to the hospital for a full checkup."

"Doc Finney let you deliver?"

"Yes. I'd forgotten what a rush that could be." The wonder and satisfaction in his voice and on his face were unmistakable.

She wanted him to leave so she could get her robe. Otherwise, she was going to have to sit here with her arms folded until she regained control of her involuntary muscles. Her nipples were as hard as pencil erasers. "You won't be delivering any babies in cardiology."

"No, I guess not." He put Josh on the floor. The sadness in his eyes made her breath catch. "Delivering Sandra's baby made me wish I could have been there for Josh's birth."

Unshed tears clogged her throat and burned her eyes. "Maybe you'll be there for your next child."

"Since I can't handle this one, I'm not making plans for another one."

Josh made a beeline for a pile of boxes in the corner, crawling as fast as his short limbs would carry him. He pulled himself up on a box, and the one stacked on top of it wobbled. Tracy shot to her feet and raced across the room to catch it before it could fall on him.

Cort did the same and they had a near collision. He caught her around the waist with one arm and steadied the boxes with the other. Her nipples prodded his chest, and his groin pressed against her belly. The thin layers of fabric did nothing to disguise the length and heat of his flesh as it twitched to life against her. Her insides fused into one tight achy knot.

The sharp whistle of his breath between his teeth made her glance up. He held her at arm's length and ran his gaze over her as thoroughly as a touch. Her skin prickled in its wake. She felt both hot and cold, as if someone had rubbed mentholated oil all over her. She didn't need a Master's degree to conclude that the dormer window behind her had probably made her old nightie transparent, and then there were those eraser-tipped breasts of hers that he'd have to be in a coma to miss.

"Trace?" His voice was as rough as pine bark and his gaze as hot as a bonfire. He swallowed hard, visibly, and his bare chest rose and fell as he took a deep breath and exhaled slowly. She ducked her head to avoid the hot question in his eyes, but his scrub pants said it all.

Dear Lord. It was bad enough that she had to fight her own illogical desire. Could she fight his, too?

"We have to quit meeting like this." His whispered attempt at humor fell flat, but he didn't release her. Instead, his fingers tightened and the sensitive skin of her waist caught fire.

His dark eyes locked with hers, and she couldn't catch her breath. "Good idea," she wheezed.

His gaze dropped to her mouth. "Are you going to deck me the way you decked Bobby Smith in tenth grade if I kiss you?"

A flicker of shame diminished the fire in her chest. "Probably not."

The corner of his mouth tipped up. She knew because she couldn't take her eyes off his lips. "Probably?"

"He offered me money, Cort, to kiss more than his lips."

Cort swore and hugged her close. His skin scorched through her nightgown from knees to shoulders, and she trembled. "Remind me to kick his ass the next time I see him."

He nudged her chin upward with his knuckle and dipped his head. Her mouth went as dry as a desert a split second before he covered her lips with his. This wasn't a tentative brotherly brush like before. This time Cort took possession. He coaxed and teased with lips and tongue until she thought she might need CPR. Her hands were trapped between them. She curled and flexed her fingers against his chest, threading through his sparse hair and then flattening her hands against the wall of muscle. His heart pounded beneath her palm, and hers raced to catch up.

The warmth of his palms skated down her back and over her thin gown to cup her hips and pull her flat against the thick ridge of his erection. She gasped at the soldering contact, and he took advantage by flicking the slick blade of his tongue against hers.

Cort wanted her. A man could fake a lot of things, but the pulsing heat pressed against her belly wasn't one of them. Her knees weakened and her skin flushed. With swishes and swirls, strokes and sweeps he teased and tormented her mouth, inviting her to play along.

And she wanted to play. She lifted her hands to his shoulders and kneaded the tightly packed muscles beneath his warm, supple skin. As passion coiled in her belly, a new tenderness entered her breasts, and a neediness she'd never known blossomed inside her.

Suddenly Libby's insane idea for Tracy to seduce

Cort seemed perfectly…well, *sane,* but she wouldn't do it to coerce him into staying. Forever wasn't in the cards for them, but maybe she could have him for the summer, and then she'd have the memory of making love with Cort to keep her warm when she was an old maid with forty cats.

Cort eased back a smidgen. Their ragged breaths mingled. Looking as stunned as she felt, he let his hands fall to his sides and then shoved a shaky hand through his hair. He glanced at Josh and then back at her. "Woman, you pack a wallop."

A laugh born of tension and pleasure bubbled out. She inhaled slowly, deeply. "There could be more where that came from…if you're willing."

His shoulder muscles tensed beneath her fingers, and she lowered her hands. His eyes narrowed and he straightened. "Exactly what are you suggesting, Tracy Sullivan?"

She wet her lips, gathered her courage and knotted her fingers. "I'm not looking for a husband. You're not looking for a wife, but we're both adults with—" heat prickled her skin "—needs. We could, um, explore those."

He blinked. How could she have forgotten the man had lashes the average woman would kill to call her own? "Are you propositioning me?"

Was it too late to crawl under the rug? Josh scampered around her feet. She'd bet he had no clue that his nanny was making a fool of herself. He tugged on her hem and pulled to stand. The resulting cool draft on her hot skin reminded her that she didn't have a stitch on beneath her gown, and she felt exposed in more ways than one.

What if Cort turned her down? How would she face him each day for the rest of the summer? "I'm suggesting that perhaps we could fulfill those needs for each other."

For several seconds he just looked at her. "You know I'm leaving in a couple of months and you still want to sleep with me?"

She lifted her chin and cursed her scalding cheeks. "Yes, and then we'll say goodbye until the next ten-year reunion."

He rubbed the back of his neck. "What about your neighbors? Your reputation? The principal job?"

If word got out that she was having a torrid affair, then not only would folks have more bad things to say about her family, she could kiss the job goodbye.

"As long as we use the inside stairs and keep this between the two of us, no one will know." She rolled one shoulder. The strap of her gown slipped down to her elbow.

Cort's gaze fastened on newly revealed flesh. His finger scraped against her upper arm as he dragged the fabric back in place. She shivered, and goose bumps popped out on her skin. "You're sure about this? You wouldn't rather have some guy who could give you the ring, the white picket fence and the whole nine yards?"

"I already have a picket fence, and I told you before, I don't plan to have children. That means I don't need the ring and the rest." She smoothed her damp palms against her gown.

Several tense moments passed before Cort said, "Yes."

Her heart beat so hard she feared she would burst an eardrum. *Yes,* he'd sleep with her or *yes,* if word got out she could kiss the job goodbye? "Could you, um, expand on that a bit?"

A naughty grin turned up the corners of his mouth, and mischief danced in his eyes. "Trace, if I expand any more I'm going to rupture a blood vessel."

She pressed her left hand to her chest and struggled to catch her breath. She would not look at his erection. Instead she offered her right hand. "Well, all right, then. We're in agreement."

Cort curled his long fingers around hers and lifted her hand to his mouth. His breath and then his lips whispered across her knuckles. Her knees wobbled.

"We have a deal, and you'd better hold on to your shorts, Ms. Sullivan, because it's going to be a long, *hot* summer."

Four

"**D**adada."

Cort's racing heart shuddered to a stop and then stumbled back into rhythm. He jerked his attention from Tracy's flushed face and swollen lips to Josh on the floor at his feet. The transition from hungry man to inexperienced father wasn't a smooth one. He sucked in a deep breath and then swallowed hard.

His son stared up at him with one tiny hand latched on to his scrubs and the other clinging to Tracy's gown. "Dadada."

An invisible brawler put a fist in his gut, knocking the air from his lungs and sapping the strength from his legs. "Is he talking to me or just practicing sounds?"

Tracy snatched her hand from his, knotted her fingers at her waist and switched into teacher mode. He didn't know how she did it, but there was something about her posture and the tilt of her head that shouted she was in charge. It turned him on. "The average nine-month-old recognizes and identifies his father as Dada."

He grinned, liking the contradiction of the stilted way she stood and talked when just seconds ago she'd been soft, pliant and hot against him. He crouched to scoop up Josh. His son's tiny fist held on to Tracy's hem, dragging it upward when he straightened. He caught a glimpse of her long, sleekly muscled thighs before Tracy quickly freed the fabric. Thighs he would soon be touching.

Oh, man. If he got any harder he'd be able to hammer nails.

How long would it be before Josh took a nap?

Then it hit him like a dousing with ice water. He wasn't prepared. Dammit. "Trace, I don't have any protection. I'm clean and I'm sure you are, but I won't take any chances on an unplanned pregnancy."

Hell, after Kate he didn't know if he'd ever have unprotected sex again—no matter how exclusive the relationship or what the woman said about being on the pill. "Did you lay in a supply of condoms when you cooked up this idea?"

Her mouth opened and closed a couple of times, and her cheeks turned scarlet. Her gaze never rose above his chin. "I have not been plotting. My decision was an impulsive one."

His belly sank as if he'd just plunged down the incline of a roller coaster. "You want to reconsider?"

"No, but we can't buy the condoms in town. Everyone would know…"

The community grapevine. Folks would know their plans before he could get home with his purchase. "I'll drive over to the pharmacy in Loma Alta."

Her hand covered her throat, but he could see her

pulse pounding between her long, slender fingers. Fingers that would soon stroke his skin, wrap around him. Heat curled in his abdomen. He cleared his throat.

"That, um, sounds fine."

"Tracy, if you're not sure about this—"

"I am." She squared her shoulders. "Now perhaps you'll give Josh to me and get dressed for work."

"I have time. You go ahead." He caught her hand and pressed his lips to the pads of her fingertips. "And, Trace, when your hands are slick with soap and sliding over your skin, know that I'm wishing they were mine."

When she heard Cort's truck pull into the drive Tracy's hands shook so badly she had to lay down the spatula or risk splattering dinner across the stovetop.

She smoothed her hair, knotted her trembling fingers and then smoothed her hair again. She'd spent Josh's nap time preparing for Cort and wishing she'd paid more attention when Libby talked at length about her assorted beauty rituals. Calling and asking her friend to explain them again was out of the question because she didn't want to draw attention to her situation or— heaven forbid—have Libby broadcast her relationship with Cort across the county.

Primping today made absolutely no sense since Cort had called and told her his schedule wouldn't permit a side trip to Loma Alta today. They wouldn't become intimate tonight. Regardless, she'd shaved her legs, plucked her brows and slathered lotion all over herself. As a result her skin was overly sensitive, and the friction of her favorite sundress stimulated her unbearably each time it swished across her thighs or scraped her breasts.

Scooping Josh off the floor she made her way to the front door. Cort covered the length of the walk in a few long strides, looking so polished and handsome in his navy-blue suit that her stomach did cartwheels. "Daddy's home."

Josh didn't hide his face in her neck, but neither did he reach for Cort when the screen door opened. After a moment's hesitation, Cort swept a hand over Josh's head. "Hey, buddy."

Cort stepped inside, closed the heavy wooden front door and leaned against it. He loosened his red tie, unfastened the top two buttons of his shirt and then cupped a hand around her waist to pull her close. Their thighs touched, and her heart nearly tumbled out of her chest.

He feathered a kiss on her forehead, her nose and, finally, her mouth. The kiss ended much too quickly—just about the time she recovered from the shocking need to stroke the dark hair in his open collar and decided to participate in Cort's kiss.

"Hey, Trace. How was your day?" The corner of his mouth tilted up and mischief warred with heat in his dark eyes.

He'd just scattered her wits and he expected her to carry on a coherent conversation? Exhaling slowly, she put a few inches between them and struggled to construct a sentence. "Josh and I had a good day. And yours?"

He grimaced, but his gaze never left hers. "Frustrating. I kept thinking about coming home and tasting you."

Her mouth dropped open and she forgot to breathe. She nearly dissolved into a puddle on the hardwood floor of her foyer. Josh squirmed in her arms, bringing her out of her stupor. She snapped her mouth closed and set him on the floor. He scampered off toward the toys she'd unpacked and piled on a quilt in the corner of the den.

She wanted to fan herself, but fisted her hands by her sides instead. "Yes, well, I was actually inquiring about your patients."

Amusement crinkled the skin around his eyes. "My hands are tied. I'm limited in what I can do until my license to practice comes through. Doc Finney has to supervise every decision I make and sign every prescription I write. That's frustrating, too. Guess I'm just a frustrated guy." He rocked back on his heels.

His wink had her stomach doing all kinds of anatomically impossible tricks. Before she had an inkling of what he planned, he pulled the clip from her hair, and the cool strands tumbled over her shoulders. He finger combed out the tangles. His obvious pleasure dammed her protest, sent a shiver down her spine and warmed her from the inside out.

"I like your hair long."

Breathe. "Yes, well, I never actually intended to grow it out. I just never have time for a haircut even though Amy's always nagging me to do something with it. She's a hairstylist now." Biting her tongue, she glanced toward the kitchen. Dear Lord, she was blathering like an idiot. "I should check on dinner."

"I'm glad you haven't let your sister cut your hair. It's sexy. Makes a man anticipate the feel of it dragging across his bare chest. And elsewhere."

His predatory smile and the desire in his eyes made her breath catch. Had she unleashed an animal? Would Cort torment her this way right up until they made love? She didn't think she could endure days of verbal foreplay.

"I..." Her mind turned to mush and her voice cracked. She swallowed and tried again. "The scampi is going to scorch, and the noodles are going to boil over."

The pasta wasn't the only thing in danger of boiling over. Without another word she bolted for the kitchen as fast as her weak knees would carry her.

Cort grinned at her retreating back. He shouldn't enjoy teasing her so much, but watching the flush spread from her cheeks down her neck and across her chest was one hell of a turn-on. Her pupils dilated until they nearly obscured her golden-brown irises, and if she breathed any harder she'd blow a seam on her very sexy sundress. He enjoyed every twitch of her bottom in the swishy yellow fabric as she beat a hasty retreat. And those legs... He took a calming breath and ran an unsteady hand through his hair.

Who'd have thought he and Tracy would ever become intimate? Back in high school she'd ridden him harder than any of his teachers. She'd bullied and threatened him, but she'd always made him strive to be the best he could be. Not once had she shown any inclination that she wanted any relationship other than tutor/student.

When her brother, David, told him she didn't have a prom date he'd volunteered his services and invited her the next day. He liked Tracy because she'd always accepted him the way he was without trying to change him. She wouldn't complain if he couldn't afford a fancy dinner or a tux.

Prom night had started off great. They'd had dinner at her favorite barbecue place in Tilden. It wasn't fancy, but it was better than her kitchen or his, the only other places they'd eaten together. The evening had continued to go well after they reached the gym, but then about an hour or two into the dance Tracy had returned from the ladies' room claiming to have a headache and asking to be taken home. The next day she'd been as stiff as an iceberg and just about as warm. Something had gone wrong, and he'd never found out what. School had ended and they'd parted ways.

But that was then. Now they were two consenting adults, and since neither of them expected more than a pleasurable summer out of this affair, then neither of them would be disappointed as long as they were discreet.

He tossed his coat and tie on the back of a chair, rolled up his sleeves and crossed the room to sit on the edge of the quilt beside Josh. "I think she likes us, buddy."

Josh hugged a stuffed puppy and stared up at him with a serious expression. Cort's gaze drifted over the toys Tracy had unpacked. "We're going to have to take care of this stuff. It's all you'll ever have from your mom."

He fingered the St. Christopher medal hanging around his own neck. It was the only thing he had from the woman who'd given birth to him and then abandoned him.

"I packed your mother's things real carefully. Your uncle Patrick's going to store them for you at Crooked Creek, and one day when you're older we'll go through everything together."

A sound made him turn his head. Tracy stood in the archway blinking rapidly with her fingers pressed to her lips. She lowered her hand. "Dinner's ready."

Her tears made his throat tighten. "Hear that, kid? It's time for grub."

He swung Josh into the air. A noise that sounded suspiciously like a laugh stopped him in his tracks. He swung his son into the air again and Josh rewarded him with a gurgle. "Progress, buddy. We might make it after all."

Tracy looked up from the dish she'd set on the table. "Of course you will. You've never failed at anything you wanted."

"I couldn't keep my mother from leaving." Whoa. Where in the hell had that come from? Kate's death had resurrected all kinds of emotions he thought he'd buried, but the last thing he needed to do was ruin the night by dragging up depressing stuff like being dumped by the only two women he'd loved in his life.

"Cort, you were two years old."

"Yes, but…" Tracy was the only one he trusted enough to voice the doubts that had always haunted him. "Was I such a horrible kid that she couldn't bear to be around me? Did I drive her away? Was I the final straw on the camel's back?"

She stepped closer and laid a hand on his arm, scorching him with her touch. "You should talk to your father."

"I did. He claims she left because of him."

"That's what Libby says, too."

A humorless laugh escaped his lips. "The McMullen County grapevine."

She grimaced and returned to the stove. "It's faster than the cable news network, and Patrick's illegitimacy supports the fact that your parents weren't happy even before you were born."

"I wish I could have stayed around for him when the news of his parentage hit the fan."

"It was as big as an alien landing, but he and Leanna

handled it well, and he's been very generous to the community since inheriting his birth father's millions.''

He strapped Josh into his high chair and sat down. Tracy leaned over him to set his dinner in front of him. The aroma of the shrimp, butter and garlic made his mouth water, but the sweep of her soft hair against her nape made his gut clench and refocused his thoughts on his baser desires.

"I'm glad you saved Kate's belongings for Josh."

He shrugged and tried to think of something besides tangling his fingers in her hair and kissing her until neither one of them could remain vertical. "She left everything to him. I donated her clothes to a women's shelter, but it didn't feel right to sell the rest without him knowing what he had first."

He lifted his fork and then set it back down. Their hunger couldn't be assuaged tonight—not in the way he'd hoped, but that didn't mean he hadn't made plans.

"Tracy, Doc Finney gave me a schedule today. With the virus that's going around he wants me working most of the daylight hours for the next couple of weeks. Does the Loma Alta pharmacy still keep banker's hours and close on Sunday?"

"Yes."

"Could you pick up the condoms?"

She stared at him with wide eyes. "Um, certainly."

She sounded as if she'd rather run naked down Main Street.

He narrowed his eyes. "Have you ever bought condoms?"

He couldn't believe how uncomfortable she was. "No."

"I'll change my schedule."

"No. I can handle this. A responsible woman takes

care of herself." She took a slow breath and exhaled, looking as though she'd braced herself for the removal of a big splinter. "Josh and I will go shopping tomorrow."

The creak of Cort's tread descending the stairs caused Tracy's heart to skip a beat.

Tomorrow, tomorrow, tomorrow. They wouldn't make love until she made the necessary purchase, and oh, Lord, she was not looking forward to that. So why, if nothing was going to happen tonight, was her heart racing out of control, and why had a flock of big honking geese taken flight in her stomach?

Cort had changed out of his suit and into faded jeans and a snug white T-shirt, reminding her of the high school boy she'd once adored, but the man oozed sex appeal in a way the boy never had. His feet were bare and his hair smooth, as if he'd taken the time to comb it.

"Did Josh finally fall asleep?"

"Yes, about ten minutes ago." He crossed the room, took the magazine from her hand and tossed it onto the coffee table.

Alarmed, she sat up straighter. "What are you doing?"

The predatory look in his eyes made her mouth dry and her palms damp. "*We're* going to make out on your sofa."

Her lungs went on strike. "But…but we don't have protection."

He settled snugly beside her, curling his arm around her shoulders. His thigh pressed hers and his rib cage seared her arm. His cologne and hint of shaving cream teased her senses. He'd shaved away his five-o'clock shadow. Oh, Lord.

A slow, wicked grin—the kind that would have fathers locking their doors and loading their shotguns—curved his lips. "We won't need condoms tonight."

Pulling her even closer, he paused with his mouth a scant inch from hers. His minty breath warmed her lips. "If you're not interested, all you have to do is say so."

She bit her bottom lip. "I am."

"Good, because, Trace, I've been thinking about this all day." He cradled her face in one big, hot palm and kissed her—the slow-burning kind of kiss that made her glad she was already seated. Her knees wouldn't have withstood such a sensual assault of soft lips, slick tongue and hungry male.

He sipped and seduced until she opened for him and invited him deeper. The dance of his tongue against hers caused her stomach to flutter and her muscles to tighten.

She didn't know what to do with her hands, but she was certain she ought to put them…somewhere. Her thoughts drifted off as his mouth scorched her jaw, her neck, her collarbone. She gasped when he nuzzled her cleavage and his breath steamed her flesh. Oh, my.

He drew back a fraction, trapping her with his smoldering dark eyes. "Have you ever made out on a couch?"

Breathe. "No."

He drew back farther in surprise. "That's un-American."

The haze of arousal dimmed. "I was the class brainiac, remember? I wasn't flooded with date invitations."

"Teenage boys have never been known for being the brightest folks on the planet, but surely when you went away to college…?"

The last flicker of arousal died, and her cheeks heated with shame. She'd been so busy helping her overworked parents raise her siblings that many of the rites of passage other folks took for granted had passed her by. When she'd finally made it to college, she'd studied her fanny off to keep from losing her scholarship and her only opportunity for an education.

"I didn't go away to college. I lived at home and commuted to the University of Texas in Kingsville."

Cort sat back. His stunned expression said it all. "Trace, you're not a virgin, are you?"

She wished she could lie, but lying wasn't her nature. "Yes."

He stood, shoved his hands into his pockets and paced to her bay window. She'd drawn the curtains at sunset, so he wasn't there for the view.

"You need to reconsider this summer fling thing," he said without looking at her.

She eyed the tense line of his shoulders with resignation. "No, Cort, I don't. I know every eligible male in this community, and I have no inclination to become intimate with any of them. You, on the other hand, I trust. We've known each other forever, but I also know you're leaving, so I won't be reminded that you've seen me naked each time I bump into you at the grocery store."

He turned. Doubt etched his features. "But, Tracy—"

His rejection stung, and her eyes burned. She pushed off the sofa and shoved her feet into her sandals, determined to escape to the solitude of her bedroom before she did something stupid like cry. "Forget I asked. I realize most men consider virgins the equivalent of a communicable disease."

Cort stepped into her path. "Tracy, it's not that."

"Forget it. I'd probably only disappoint you, anyway." She mashed her quivering lips together, clenched her teeth and tried to step around him.

His steps mirrored hers, blocking her escape. Lifting his hand he brushed her cheek with a gentle finger and tipped her chin until she met his gaze. "This is not something you can undo once it's done."

A sob built in her throat at the tenderness in his dark eyes. "I know that, but I'm twenty-eight years old, and, Cort, you're the only man I've ever met who makes me feel feminine and sexy instead of like a geeky schoolteacher."

One corner of his mouth tipped up in a lopsided, boyish smile. "Then, Miss Sullivan, please allow me the privilege of being *your* tutor for a change."

Her stomach dropped to her feet.

She stood there like a rag doll while he lifted her arms and looped them around his neck, and then he cupped her waist and eased closer. One step, two, until their thighs and bellies touched. "If I do anything you don't like or if I move to fast, speak up or pop me upside the head—whatever works for you."

A smile trembled on her lips. "You don't have to—"

He cut off her words with a quick kiss. "I want to make love with you, Trace."

He pulled her forward until her breasts, braless in her halter-necked sundress, pressed against the hard wall of his chest. His warmth permeated the thin layers of fabric, and her nipples hardened as if he'd caressed them with his hands. Just the thought of him touching her so intimately made her insides quiver and her mind turn to mush.

Think. Concentrate on what you're supposed to be doing.

She flexed her fingers in indecision. Men, according to the articles she'd read, like to be touched, too. But where exactly? She tangled her fingers in Cort's short hair. The soft strands teased her palms in a distracting way, and then he kissed her and her focus blurred. She ran her hands over the tightly packed muscles of his shoulders and down his back, but her movements were awkward and jerky.

He lifted his mouth from hers long enough to suck in a sharp breath and let it out on a groan. Good, at least one of them was enjoying this.

Concentrate. He kissed her again, harder, deeper. She'd memorized a map locating a man's erogenous zones, but the picture grew hazy and then vanished completely when he suckled her tongue. Lordy, the man knew how to kiss, and if he kept that up she'd never remember what she was supposed to do to please him.

He widened his stance and pulled her into the cradle of his thighs, incinerating her brain cells. She'd once read an article about seducing your man, but when Cort's hands stroked over her bottom, pressing the ridge of his arousal against her sensitive flesh, she couldn't recall one single detail.

Think. Where were her hands supposed to be? They weren't supposed to hang at her side like dried spaghetti the way they did now, and if she dug her nails any farther into her palms she'd need first aid.

Cort pulled back, pinning her with his dark gaze. "Trace, how many research books have you read about making love?"

Not enough, obviously. "A half dozen or so. Why?"

He nodded as if her answer didn't surprise him. "Because you're thinking too hard."

Embarrassment scalded her skin. She'd bet even her

toes blushed. She struggled to get free, but instead of releasing her, his hands tightened on her waist.

"Relax. You're as tense as a bowstring," he instructed in a deep, hypnotic voice against her temple. "Concentrate on how it feels when my fingers glide across your skin."

As if she could think about anything else.

"Making love is about feeling, not thinking."

She jerked to attention. "But we're not going to make love."

His grin weakened her knees, and she had to cling to his forearms or risk collapsing at his feet. "Correction, teach. We're not going to hit a home run, but we are going to have one hell of a good time running the bases."

Dear heaven. His words sent shock waves through her.

He kissed her lids closed, then her gaping mouth. "Close your eyes, Trace, and feel."

She focused on his masculine scent, his touch, and on the texture of his hands as he stroked from the crown of her head, over her bare shoulders, down her spine, to the swell of her hips and back again until a shiver raced over her.

"You have goose bumps." Warm breath stirred the tendrils around her ear. His lips brushed her earlobe seconds before he caught the sensitive skin in his teeth. "Do you know how arousing it is for me to know I caused them?"

Did he have any clue how arousing it was for her to have them? He'd sensitized her skin to the point that even the brush of her own hair against her shoulder blades tormented her.

He strung kisses along her jaw and down the side of

her neck, and then he traced an erotic pattern on her shoulder with his hot tongue. The scrape of his teeth made her moan. She bit her lip and cringed.

He freed the tender skin with his thumb and waited until her eyes fluttered open and she met his gaze. "Don't. I want to know when I please you. Or if I don't."

He carried her hand to his lips and pressed an open-mouthed kiss against her palm. The swirl of his tongue made her gulp.

Cort led her to the sofa, sat down and pulled her across his lap. His arousal pressed against her hip, and a hollow ache opened up low in her belly. His chest warmed her arm, and she burrowed closer.

He half groaned, half whispered into her ear, "Close your eyes again."

As soon as she did, the featherlight touch of his fingertips traced her hairline, her brows, her nose. He outlined her cheekbones, her jawline and her lips. His thumb nudged her lips apart to tease the delicate skin inside, and just when she developed an urge to open her mouth and taste him, he moved on to trace the shell of her ear and the tendons of her neck. Not knowing where he'd touch next amplified her reactions.

One finger followed the halter strap of her dress from the knot at her nape on a downward path toward her breastbone. She gasped for breath and her nipples hardened in anticipation of his touch. She arched her back, but Cort ignored the invitation and skimmed upward on the opposite side.

When he reached the knot at her nape again he tugged, and the fabric slackened but didn't fall. On his downward quest he edged his fingertips beneath the strap drawing closer and closer to her breasts. Breathing became more difficult, but she wasn't the only one panting. The exhilarating proof that touching her turned him on scorched her hip, and his rapid exhalations swept her neck and shoulder, stirring her hair.

"You feel good, Trace. Your skin is so soft."

As if his touch weren't overwhelming enough, he leaned her back against the end of the sofa and kissed her. One long, slow, drugging kiss melted into another. Her head spun. She tangled her fingers in his hair and held on. When his hand dipped inside her top to cup her breast she nearly inhaled him with her gasp. His palm was hot and her breast so sensitive that she could feel each of his fingers curled around her flesh.

He lifted his head and held her gaze as his thumb brushed over her tight, achy nipple. Dear heavens.

The banked fire in his eyes burned her up. "Okay?"

She could barely nod, let alone speak. The tingles from his touch reached deep down inside her, knotting her insides, warming her body and making her crave more. More of his touch. More of his kisses. He rolled her sensitive skin between his thumb and finger, and a moan slipped free. He nudged aside the fabric of her top, uncovering her.

She bit her lip, afraid he'd be disappointed. She wasn't exactly Pamela Anderson. He lowered his head before she could gauge his expression and engulfed her with his hot, moist mouth.

Pleasure so intense it nearly propelled her off the sofa swelled within her. She tightened her fingers in his hair, and a needy sound squeezed past her lips. He suckled, licked and nipped her, and she caught fire. It's a wonder she didn't scorch a hole through his lap. As it was, she couldn't sit still, and her squirming made him groan against her.

"Cort, *please*." She had no idea what she was begging him to do, but she wanted him to do something to ease the tension inside her before she snapped like an overstretched rubber band.

He didn't seem to face the same confusion. His hand left her breast and curled around her ankle. *Her ankle?* She'd never read anywhere that touching the spot between her Achilles tendon and her anklebone would make her leg muscles quiver. His hand moved upward in butterfly-soft strokes as his mouth moved to lavish attention on her opposite breast.

She raked her fingers from his hair down his spine, pulling him closer. Liking the satisfied sound he made, she ran her short nails up his back again, and then she traced his ear, the way he'd done hers.

"Mmm," he murmured against her skin. The sound vibrated all the way to her toes.

Cort kissed her again, this time harder, as if he wanted to consume her. When his hand slipped beneath her hem, she almost bit his tongue. He lifted his head and held her gaze as his fingers found her damp panties and drew ever-shrinking circles over the center of her desire. She trembled in his arms.

He eased his hand beneath the elastic and found her slick and ready. Her breath shuddered in and out. All conscious thought focused on the way he plied her, sweeping her higher and higher until release rocked her. Her muscles tensed and her back bowed as she jerked in his arms and called his name.

He kissed her brow, nuzzled her lips, her throat, her ear. Before she could become embarrassed over her noisy pleasure, he dipped his head and sipped at her breasts, beginning the torment all over again. This time the explosion came quicker. In only seconds he had her gasping and arching, pressing shamelessly into his hand.

With her hunger somewhat satisfied, she wanted to return the favor. Pulling him close she devoured his mouth with the hunger he'd taught her, but he stiffened in her arms. She thought she'd offended him with her aggressiveness until Josh's cry penetrated her passionate haze.

Cort leaned his forehead against hers, and their panting breaths mingled. "Guess that's the end of lesson one, and that's a damned shame, because lesson two looks real interesting."

Holding her in his arms, he stood and then he laid her on the sofa and pressed a quick, hard kiss to her mouth. "Sleep well, Trace."

She clutched her top over her nakedness and sat up. "What about you?"

Despite the strain in his features he winked. "Tomorrow."

Cort left her with her newfound knowledge and a hunger to bring him the pleasure he'd brought her. Rather than dreading the trip to the pharmacy, she could hardly wait to get there.

Five

Cort ranked touching Tracy, tasting her and having her come apart in his arms right up there with a class-three narcotic in the addictive category. He wanted another dose. His pulse accelerated in anticipation of watching the wonder in her eyes and hearing the catch in her breath as he led her through new territory.

He stopped by the reception desk, handed Doc Finney a patient's file for review and did a quick head count of the waiting room. A few more patients to see and he could leave.

The clinic's front door flew open and a man rushed inside. "Doc, there's a bad wreck out on Highway 16. High school football team was heading to a scrimmage. Some jerk T-boned 'em at the intersection. Bus rolled."

Doc Finney tossed the files onto the desk. "We're closer than the paramedics. Pam, hand me my bag." He turned to Cort. "Get bandages and antiseptic—anything we might need on the scene."

Cort's adrenaline kicked in. He jogged back to the supply room and found a large box. The small county clinic was a far cry from the first-class facility where he'd been training. The furniture and equipment were old. The clinic wasn't as well equipped or organized as the E.R., and the supplies were pitifully low, but he gathered what he could and headed for the front desk. If Patrick wanted to throw his money around, then he'd put a bug in his brother's ear about donating to Doc's clinic.

"Pam, could you call Tracy and tell her I'll be late and why?" he called out as he jogged past the reception desk.

"Will do, Cort."

One look at Cort's torn and bloodstained suit and Tracy's heart dropped to her stomach.

She jerked upright on the sofa, tossed off the quilt and then catapulted to her feet. "Cort, are you all right?"

"Blood's not mine." He looked exhausted. His hair was a mess. "Josh—?"

"He's sleeping. Is Chuck okay? I couldn't get Libby on the phone." Cort's battered appearance led her to believe that the accident had been every bit as bad as the grapevine reported.

"He was standing in the aisle going over plays with the kids when the bus overturned. He broke a few bones and took a blow to the head that the docs want to keep an eye on, but his prognosis is good. Libby's at the hospital with him."

"What about the boys?"

"No casualties, but a few of them won't play ball again anytime soon." Defeat tightened his voice.

She wanted to pull him into her arms, but resisted the impulse. "I'm sure you did the best you could."

"We kept them stable until the ambulances arrived."

"And then you followed the ambulances to the hospital, waited with the parents until they received the news, *and* you translated the medical jargon for them."

He grimaced. "The grapevine."

"Yes. You can't sniffle here without folks showing up at your door with chicken soup. They mean well. Do you want me to try to clean and repair your suit?"

He looked down and shook his head. "Lost cause. Just find me a garbage bag."

"Go take a hot shower. I'll reheat your dinner."

He started for the stairs and stopped. "Tracy, I'm sorry about tonight. Maybe later we can—"

Her heart ached with disappointment, but she folded her arms and gave him her teacher's you've-got-to-be-kidding-me look. "Cort, you're dead on your feet, and I doubt you're in the mood to…"

"Rock your world?"

Her entire body flushed with heat. "Uh, yes. Perhaps we'd best save that for another time. Now, please go. I'll bring up a trash bag."

She put his dinner in the microwave, grabbed a garbage bag and climbed the stairs. The bathroom door opened as soon as she entered his bedroom, and Cort stepped out wearing only a towel slung low around his hips. Her breath wedged in her chest.

Droplets of water clung to his hair and skin. Her gaze tracked one as it glided past his St. Christopher medallion, over his pectorals and abdomen to be absorbed into the white terry cloth. She felt as if her hormones—

which had simmered all day in anticipation of being in his arms tonight—bubbled in her veins.

"Tracy?" The innuendo in his voice said her expression had revealed too much.

She blew out a slow breath and shook out the plastic bag. "Drop in your suit and I'll carry it downstairs."

He turned back to the steam-filled room, gathered the ruined garments and dumped them into the bag.

"Dinner can wait." His rough whisper combined with his knuckle scraping along her cheekbone nearly caused her knees to buckle.

She stepped out of reach even though she yearned for his touch. "No, Cort, it can't. It's after midnight. You have to be up in six hours, and we both know Josh will get up at least once tonight. Please, let's wait until we won't be rushed."

She cursed her telling redhead's skin.

A smile of sensual promise tilted one corner of his mouth. "Sounds good to me, 'cause sweetheart, I want to have the time and energy to savor every inch of you."

Tracy turned, praying her knees were strong enough to keep her from tumbling headfirst down the stairs.

Cort's heart, anticipating an evening of fun and games, kicked into overdrive the moment Tracy opened the front door. Her summery dress made him think of sizzling heat, skinny-dipping and her slick skin sliding against his. She'd worn her hair loose—just the way he liked.

The picnic basket looped over her arm threw him. "Are you planning to take me out into the countryside and have your way with me, Ms. Sullivan?"

She waved him inside. "Run upstairs and change while I put this in the car."

He kissed Josh's forehead and reached for her.

She dodged, but she wet her lips. "None of your shenanigans. You'll make us late."

"Late for what?"

She folded her arms and gave him a look that made him feel like he'd forgotten to raise his hand. "You forgot about your father and Penny's anniversary party, didn't you?"

Damn. "Yes."

Instead of him and Tracy alone and tangled in the sheets, he'd be surrounded by family and food. He took Josh from her and winced when his son tried to twist his nose off his face. He captured those strong little fingers.

"I have strict instructions to bring you, or else."

"Or else what?" Maybe they could leave early.

"You'll have to ask your brothers. Each of them called to make sure you'd be there."

No dodging family obligations. With a frustrated sigh he hooked an arm around her waist and pulled her close. "Are we on for later? You. Me. Moonlight and bare skin?"

Her shuddery breath pressed her breasts against his side. She lifted her chin, looking all prim and proper, but the yearning in her eyes and the flush tinting her skin told another story. "We'll see."

His groin throbbed in anticipation. "I need a kiss to give me the strength to get through my shower."

She laughed and danced out of his arms. "You are so full of it my students could take lessons from you."

Cort stroked her cheek and winked. "Anticipation is half the fun. And, Trace, I'm anticipating tasting you right here.'' He brushed his finger across her lips and then traced a path over her collarbone to one breast. Her nipple peaked. "And here." He bisected her belly.

Her eyes widened and her color deepened. She took a hasty step back. "Yes, well, you'd better get ready— if you want to get home at a reasonable hour."

He grinned, caught her hand and pressed his lips to the pulse pounding inside her wrist. Her breath caught audibly. "I'll make it worth the wait. That's a promise, Miss Sullivan."

When had home ceased to be home?

Cort parked the truck in front of the Pink Palace rooming house that his father and stepmother owned and operated. It shamed him to admit that he could count his trips home in the past five years on one hand and have fingers to spare.

He turned in his seat to look at Tracy. He liked her, trusted and desired her. What more could a man ask for in a friend and lover? He winked. "Later."

She blushed, grabbed her picnic basket and dashed toward the already laden tables. A group of women, his brothers' wives among them, drew her into their circle. He moved slower, taking his time extricating Josh from his car seat.

He felt like an outsider, whereas Tracy fit right in. How had the distance crept up on him? Between full-time school and a part-time job, he'd had little time or money to travel, and then he'd met Kate right after his father's heart attack five years ago. She'd disliked the ranch, absolutely refused to stay in the rooming house, and she'd hated being alone on the holidays.

He surveyed the crowd, reluctant to wade in. Other than his sporadic visits, he'd been gone ten years, and there wasn't much to discuss besides the kids, the ranch and his training. He and his brothers had exhausted those topics on his first day back. The silences had been awkward.

Josh squirmed in his arms, and he realized he'd tensed up. He made a conscious effort to relax. His father waved from the corner of the yard where he manned the grill, and Cort returned the gesture. In the direct sunlight, his father looked every one of his seventy plus years. If he returned to North Carolina for another five years would his father still be around when he came back to visit?

His two oldest brothers circled the brick patio, lighting the tall torch lamps to keep the mosquitoes at bay. Brand, his third brother, spotted him and broke away from the group beside the cooler to pull him into a rib-crushing hug. Josh squirmed between them and Brand pulled back. "What's up, Doc?"

Cort groaned. "Like I don't hear that ten times a day."

Brand laughed and held up his hands. "Cut me some slack. Do you know how long I've waited to ask? Welcome home."

"Thanks." His throat tightened up. Although Brand was only six years older, he'd practically raised him after their mother left. They'd always been close, but school and distance had taken their toll.

Brand set his cowboy hat on Josh's head and played peekaboo with Josh under the brim. "It's good to have you back, bro, and hearing that you're working in the clinic where you belong makes all the sacrifices worth it."

The weight of his brother's expectations bore down on his shoulders. Brand had given up his own dreams of going to college to follow a rodeo career in order to bankroll the family ranch and to finance Cort's college education. Patrick had chipped in to cover medical school when he'd inherited money. He owed his brothers. Big-time.

"This is a temporary gig. I'm still planning to finish my residency as soon as I figure out how to juggle Josh and a resident's schedule."

His brother's smile faded. He set his hat back on his head. "You don't have to."

"I do if I want to repay the money you and Patrick have shelled out for my education. The salary I'm earning at the clinic won't do it. Even after I qualify as a surgeon it'll take years to cover what I owe you two."

Brand shook his head and tickled Josh, but Josh turned shy and buried his face in Cort's shirt. Cort pulled him close, savoring the first real sign of acceptance from his son.

"I don't want your money. If I hadn't been following the circuit I wouldn't have met Toni. This is the life I was meant to live, Cort." Brand gestured to his six-year-old twin daughters bent over a magazine at the picnic table and his three-year-old son riding a tricycle through the grass.

"I pay my debts."

Brand punched his arm. "You're not listening. Toni and the kids are the best things that ever happened to me. *I owe you*, little brother. And you can ask Patrick, but he inherited fifteen million dollars from his birth father, Cort. He's not going to miss the piddling amount he spent on you. Hell, it was a good cause."

"Right." He tried but failed to keep the sarcasm out of his voice. No matter how well things had turned out, his brothers had sacrificed for him, and pride demanded he repay them. Tracy understood. He searched the thirty or so guests until he found her in a huddle with his sisters-in-law. Her hair gleamed like firelight in the setting sun, and an evening breeze molded her dress to her legs and sweet behind.

His palms tingled in anticipation of touching her, of stroking and tasting her soft skin. In a few hours they'd be alone. Josh would be in bed. And so would they.

She turned as if sensing his scrutiny, and their eyes locked. Her expression slowly changed. Her lips parted and then the tip of her tongue swept over them. His heart rate doubled, and he had to swallow hard. He'd be her first lover, the first to teach her about passion, the first to feel her clench him in ecstasy. Desire wrapped around him, thickening the air and making him sweat.

Tracy dipped her head and fiddled with the edge of her sweater. He'd bet her cheeks had taken on a rosy glow. Did her pulse race as fast as his?

"You could do worse." Brand followed his gaze. "She's great with kids, and she's always been crazy about you."

Crazy about him? No way. They'd been friends before, and now they shared a serious case of lust, but if she wanted to keep their affair under wraps in a community this small that meant keeping secrets. He didn't like lying, especially to his family, but for Tracy's sake he would.

"She's my landlord and Josh's nanny. Nothing more."

"Then maybe you ought to change that, because she's a hell of a lot better for you than Kate was. Tracy won't try to make you ashamed of where you came from. She won't make you wear golf club clothes or change the way you talk.''

He opened his mouth to argue and closed it again. Had Kate tried to change him? Sure, she'd helped him pick out clothes, but he'd appreciated her opinion. He'd been a hick cowboy when he hit the Duke campus, and he'd taken a lot of ribbing for his clothes and accent. And yes, she'd corrected his pronunciation a few times, but he'd wanted to lose his southern twang.

"How about a beer?" Brand's question yanked him out of the past.

"Sure." He followed his brother to the cooler located right beside Tracy. As soon as he got within a yard of her, Josh dove for her, and Cort had to scramble not to drop the child.

Tracy caught Josh without hesitation. "This big group's a little overwhelming for you, isn't it, sport?"

Josh buried his face in her throat, and all Cort could think of was that he'd be doing the same in... He glanced at his watch. How long would they have to hang around? An hour? Two?

Brand looped his arm around his wife Toni's shoulders. "What are you ladies plotting?"

Caleb's wife, Brooke, spoke first. "We're not plotting. Both ranches have benefited from Tracy's referrals of disadvantaged students needing summer work. We're filling her in on how the kids are doing."

Leanna, Patrick's wife, added, "Without her to recommend trustworthy baby-sitters, we'd never get an evening out of the house with our men."

Toni grimaced. "I'm beginning to see the drawbacks of living two counties west of here."

Brand sent a hard look toward Cort. "Better two counties than half a country."

Direct hit. Cort didn't flinch, nor did he miss the light of battle flaring in Tracy's eyes.

Before he could reply, Caleb wandered over. "Am I missing something?"

Brand handed him a bottle of beer. "I'm trying to convince Cort to move home for good."

Caleb nodded. "I'll second the motion."

Tracy came to his defense. "If Cort stays in school he has a chance to study under the best cardiologist in the country. Would you want him to forfeit that opportunity?"

"No, but—" Caleb's shoulders squared. Cort recognized his brother's battle stance, but Tracy wasn't deterred.

She faced him with Josh on her hip. "Caleb, if anyone understands the pursuit of goals, you should, since you and Brooke teach goal actualization at the dude ranch."

His brother and Tracy stood toe-to-toe. "Yeah, but we need another doctor in the clinic."

"Shouldn't he be allowed to make his own choices? Live his own life? Follow his dreams?"

Brooke hooked an arm though her husband's. "Caleb, Tracy's right. This is Cort's decision."

"And it was a fine one when he only had himself to consider. Now he has the rug rat." He ruffled Josh's hair. "He needs to be near family. If he goes back to school, Josh will be six years old before we see him again. The boy will grow up not knowing us."

The words hit Cort like a fist in the gut. If he spent the next five years in school, most of Josh's childhood would be spent in day care. He hadn't even wanted a kid, so why did he feel an aching sense of loss over missing a few years of his life?

Tracy opened her mouth to continue arguing his cause, and Cort wanted to hug her for being his champion. As the youngest brother he'd grown up being bossed around, but after ten years away from home he could fight his own battles.

He touched his hand to the small of her back to get her attention. Her eyes rounded and her gaze jerked to his. "Thanks, Trace. I'll handle it from here."

Looking embarrassed, she bit her lip. "I just don't want your brothers to think they can gang up on you and browbeat you into submission."

"I think they got the message." Judging by their expressions, they'd read more into her defense than she'd intended.

Brooke scooped up her youngest son and set him in a plastic swimming pool someone had filled with colorful balls. The boy squealed, and Josh squirmed to get down and join him.

Tracy stepped away and lowered Josh into the play area. Josh clung to her with one hand and patted the balls with his other. Cort couldn't blame the kid. He missed the warmth of her against his palm already. He glanced at his watch. How much longer?

"Speaking of goals, Tracy, when will you hear about the principal position?" Brooke asked.

"The school board should make a final decision in the next few weeks."

Cort stepped closer. "If you have your heart set on being a principal, then why don't you apply to other school districts?"

Tracy straightened slowly, leaving Josh happily slapping balls. The steely determination in her eyes surprised him. "This is my home. I don't want to go anywhere else."

"There are more opportunities in counties with a higher population, and the money is bound to be better."

"Sometimes it's not about money, Cort."

His father rang the chow bell before he could ask her to elaborate or explain to her that he'd learned the hard way that money not only made the world go 'round, it opened doors. Josh held up his chubby arms for him. Cort let the matter drop and reached for his son.

Tracy followed the others to the buffet, wishing she could crawl under the picnic table. She'd taken Caleb to task like a momma bear defending her cub or at the very least a woman defending her man. If she wanted to keep her affair with Cort a secret, she'd have to be more discreet.

Needing a moment to gather her thoughts, she filled her plate from the overloaded tables and headed for a picnic table some distance away. She sat down between Brand's girls and Caleb's oldest son. Children were always less taxing than adults. Her ploy didn't work. When she looked up, Cort was heading directly for her table.

Her appetite for food faded, and hunger for Cort took its place. Bareheaded, in his white polo shirt, khaki shorts and loafers with no socks, he stood out in a sea of jeans, chambray shirts and cowboy hats. She had a hard time keeping her gaze off his muscular legs.

Cort settled across from her and grinned as if he'd deciphered her plan to avoid him and had every intention of circumventing it. Their feet tangled beneath the table. She quickly tucked hers under the bench, but not before the wiry hairs on his legs prickled against her skin and started her blood humming. His grin broadened. He glanced at his watch, her mouth and back to his watch again.

She flushed all over. "Where's Josh?"

"Penny insists on entertaining him while we eat."

Cort turned his attention to the children. "Did you all know that Ms. Sullivan teaches at the school your dads and all your uncles attended?"

Cort drew the kids into an animated discussion, but Tracy didn't join in. He didn't need her help. That left her free to focus on the "later" he'd mentioned in the car—not that her mind had strayed far from the subject. He had her so flustered it was a miracle she could string two sentences together.

In a matter of hours she and Cort would be lovers. Tension knotted her belly, and a fine sheen of perspiration broke out on her skin. She blotted her forehead with her paper napkin, and for the first time in her life she considered being rude and leaving a party early. In the past she'd always volunteered to help with cleaning up.

Her feet tangled with Cort's again. Had he removed his shoes? Was that his bare toe stroking her ankle, her calf, her—

Her heart sprinted. She slammed her knees closed.

Their eyes met, and the heat in his dark gaze nearly caused her to melt off the bench. Her nerves vibrated like a music teacher's tuning fork, and her hands trembled. More food fell from her fork and back onto her plate than made it to her mouth.

She wanted to beg him to take it easy on her because she was a novice at the game of seduction. He obviously wasn't. All he had to do was look at her and the fine hairs on her body stood up like antennae. She shook her head and gave him the eagle-eye stare she saved for her most difficult students. Neither fazed him. He continued chatting with the children and playing footsie under the table.

Who would have thought the soft skin of a man's instep could create such havoc gliding along her calf?

She consumed her meal with alarming haste—she'd probably have heartburn later—and retreated to the dessert table. Cort followed. She turned and whispered angrily, "Stop it."

"Stop what? I'm not doing anything." He looked the picture of innocence batting his long dark lashes at her. She thought her job had hardened her to phony, guiltless expressions, but his worked.

"You're looking at me." Oh, Lord, listen to her. She sounded like a petulant child.

A smile played on his lips. "You want me to stop looking at you?"

"You're flirting. If you keep it up everyone will know what's going on."

"Nothing's going on." He paused until she opened her mouth to debate the point. "Yet."

Her arguments died on her tongue at the weighty promise in that single, huskily voiced word. The slice of carrot cake she'd selected fell off the server and landed icing side down on her plate.

"I just want to stop thinking about…" Her skin burned. She looked left and right to make sure no one would overhear. *"It."*

"It?" One brow arched and mischief sparkled in his eyes.

"You know what I mean," she whispered.

"Does this mean you're about to self-destruct, too?"

She bit her lip. What was the point in denying it? "Yes."

"Ready to go home?"

"We can't leave yet."

"Sure we can. Josh looks tired. Doesn't he?"

She glanced over to the play area. Josh was having a ball and looked not the least bit tired. She lowered her chin and gave Cort a skeptical look.

He waggled his brows and nodded toward the car. "Shall we call it a night?"

What was the point of staying? She wouldn't be able to think about anything except *later*. "No. Yes. Maybe."

His slow, sexy smile dissolved what was left of her common sense and, darn his cocky hide, he knew it. He stepped closer, blocking her from the rest of the guests with his broad shoulders and dragged a finger along her jawline. "Do you have any idea how badly I want to hold you, taste you, be inside you?"

She closed her eyes and gulped. *Breathe.* "Yes, because I want that, too."

"Grab me a piece of the chocolate cake and wrap it to go. And, Trace, get a slice with a lot of icing, because I have plans for that icing—plans that include you."

Six

Tracy's heart beat as if she'd sprinted the fifteen miles between her home and the picnic instead of riding beside Cort in his truck.

Saying their goodbyes had taken an excruciatingly long time. By the time they'd made it home, Josh had indeed become tired and cranky, and in her agitated state she would never be able to settle him for bed.

Cort must have sensed as much. He brushed her aside and extricated Josh from his car seat. "I've got him. You go and do whatever it is women do before bedtime."

Her knees locked. What did women do before bedding a man? She had no idea.

Libby would know. But she couldn't call her friend. Libby had more important things to deal with as her husband recuperated from the accident. A stiff drink might help settle her fraying nerves. Alas, Tracy didn't drink, and the strongest thing in her house was an old bottle of crème de menthe.

Cort followed her into the house and stepped into her path. "Trace, don't."

She couldn't lift her eyes higher than his chin. "Don't what?"

"Don't work yourself into a lather. We'll take it slow. We can stop at any time." When she didn't answer, he leaned forward and settled his lips against hers. The velvety softness of his kiss sent her blood careening through her veins.

Josh grabbed a fistful of her hair, shocking her back to reality. "Ow."

Cort disengaged his tiny fingers. "This isn't brain surgery. Nobody's going to die if we make a mistake."

"Easy for you to say." She rubbed her scalp, not because it hurt, but because she didn't know what else to do with her hands. Was this a mistake? Would she regret taking Cort as a lover? And what if instead of satisfying her curiosity she fell in love with him again?

She wouldn't because—well, she just wouldn't. She knew he'd be leaving.

He tipped her chin until she met his gaze. "Easy for me to prove. Take a hot bath or read a book. I'll be with you as soon as I get Josh settled. With any luck it won't be long."

The banked fire in his eyes made her knees weak and inhibited her ability to breathe. When he turned and headed for the stairs she inhaled a much-needed supply of oxygen and pressed an unsteady hand to her chest. How long did she have to prepare herself for their love-making? Thirty minutes? An hour?

She dashed into her bedroom, closed her blinds and paced. Were her sheets clean? Oh, please, sheets were the least of her worries. Which nightgown would she wear? She stopped and stared at her dresser in horror. Did she even have one that wasn't threadbare? Spending money on something nobody else saw seemed wasteful, but, oh, what she'd give for one of those racy numbers Libby ordered from her *Victoria's Secret* catalog. And then she stared at her less-than-spectacular bosom and reconsidered. She didn't have what it took to fill out those seductive outfits.

Would Cort be disappointed?

Would she? She'd waited ten years for this night. Talk about great expectations.

She paused in the center of her room, inhaled and exhaled deeply three times. Calm. In control.

Who was she kidding?

Too rattled to make the nightgown decision, she dug the box of condoms out of her dresser drawer. Should she leave out just one plastic packet or the entire box? She didn't want to seem too desperate, but she didn't want to come across as apathetic either. Should she open the box or would that seem too eager? Chewing her lip, she compromised by breaking the seal and setting the box on her bedside table.

A shower. She snatched her robe from the end of the bed and dashed into the bathroom. After piling her hair on top of her head, she stepped into her claw-foot tub and under the hot spray. It skimmed over her skin like a hundred fingers, and she recalled Cort's words. *When your hands are slick with soap and sliding over your skin, know that I'm wishing they were mine.*

Her head spun, and she dropped the soap. When she bent to pick it up she knocked over her super-size bottle of shampoo. It landed on her big toe. Pain radiated up her leg, and though she'd never been one to swear, she

was sorely tempted now. She sat down in the tub and
bent her knees so she could rub the injured toe.

"Ow. Ow. Ow."

"Tracy?" The bathroom door opened after a gentle
tap. "Are you all right?"

She froze and then slowly lifted her eyes to look
through the clear shower curtain. Cort looked right back
at her.

Steam rose from the shower. The warm water beat
down on her overly sensitized skin. She couldn't have
put a sentence together if her life depended on it.

"Trace? I heard a crash." He pulled back the curtain
and turned off the shower. "Are you hurt?"

She managed to shake her head.

He took in her near-fetal position, the shampoo bottle
tipped on its side and the bar of soap beside the drain
in one glance, and then knelt beside the tub. "Let me
see."

Without the warm shower spray her skin cooled and
goose bumps rose on her arms. When she couldn't immediately comply, he pried her fingers away and studied
the toe. He probed with gentle fingers. "Does this hurt?
Can you bend it?"

"Not much. Yes." The effort it took to get those
three single-syllable words out amazed her, and it
wasn't caused by the pain, which had already subsided.
She spoke at length to rooms full of students or parents
without difficulty, but being naked in front of Cort par-
alyzed her vocal cords.

"I think it's just bruised," he diagnosed.

She could have told him that if her mind and her
mouth had cooperated. "Yes."

His brows dipped. "If you're in pain we can wait—"

"*No.*" Her haste was a little unbecoming. Her skin

heated. She cleared her throat, exhaled slowly and tried to reply with more dignity. "I don't want to wait."

"You're sure?" The concern in his eyes transformed into something else—something dark and sultry that made her stomach tighten and her breasts tingle. His pupils dilated and his chest expanded beneath his shirt when he inhaled. The white knit fabric of his polo shirt did nothing to conceal the hard points of his nipples. Her own returned the salute.

"Yes."

He must have heard her whispered reply because he leaned forward to plug the drain and then turned the water back on.

Warm water swirled around her bottom, touching tender, receptive skin and wreaking all kinds of havoc. Cort scooped up the bar of soap and moved behind her old claw-foot tub.

"Cort?" Alarmed, she tried to turn, but he caught her shoulders. The touch of his soapy hands hit her like a jolt of electricity.

He massaged her tense shoulders. "Relax. Isn't that what you're always telling me?"

How could she, with his hands rasping her flesh that way?

Cort plied the tight muscles along her neck and spine with his thumbs, working his way downward one vertebra at a time. His fingers brushed her ribs, her waist. A shiver shook her.

"Cold?" He scooped up handfuls of the warm bathwater. It rolled down her back and trickled over her front to her eraser-tipped breasts.

"Josh?" she croaked.

"Out like a light." He resumed the massage. Lower and lower his hands glided until he reached the water licking at her buttocks. Good heavens. She took one shaky breath after another. Her cinnamon-scented soap mingled with Cort's aftershave and a hint of toothpaste to stir her senses.

He set the soap on the shelf beside the tub, rinsed her back and then curled his hands over her shoulders again and pulled. She covered her breasts with her arms before leaning back against the cool wall of the tub.

"Don't." Cort's breath whispered in her ear as he leaned forward to turn off the spigot.

She didn't have to ask what he meant. It took every ounce of courage she possessed to lower her arms to her sides. Her heartbeat drummed in her ears and her toes curled.

He lathered his hands and then stroked his slick palms over her shoulders, but instead of soaping her needy breasts he concentrated his attention on her arm. She'd never known the inside of her upper arm could be so sensitive to a featherlight touch. And who would have thought washing the pale skin inside her elbow and forearm could make her shiver?

Cort washed between her fingers as if tracing the shape of her hand. The slow and simple movement was unbearably erotic. When his nails scraped over her palm a noise—half whimper, half moan—slipped through her lips.

He rinsed her and moved to the opposite shoulder. Dear heaven, if washing her arms could whip her insides into a frenzy, then she didn't stand a chance when he got down to business.

Closing her eyes tightly, she concentrated on the sensations washing over her. The tempo of Cort's breathing increased. He leaned closer. Each exhalation brushed her damp nape, causing goose bumps to chase across her flesh. Her thigh muscles trembled until her bent knees knocked together. She slowly straightened her legs.

Cort's breath whistled through his teeth. He rinsed her arm and shoulder and moved to the opposite end of the tub. His gaze burned from her pink toenails to the dark red curls between her legs, lingering on her tightly puckered breasts before moving on to her flushed cheeks. The passion in his eyes stole her breath. "You're beautiful, Trace."

Denial sprung to her lips, but she didn't voice the words because the way he looked at her made her feel beautiful, sexy and desirable.

Cort would soon be her lover. The deep aching need inside her bore no resemblance whatsoever to the superficial emotions of her high school crush, and that concerned her, but when his soap-slickened fingers worked over her instep her worries scattered like dandelion seeds in the wind and warmth gathered in her midsection. His featherlight touch teased the skin beneath her anklebone, and she bit her lip to stifle a moan. He kneaded her calf, traced a path behind her knee and slid his hands over her thigh, the outside and then the inside. Her breath shuddered in and out. Everything inside her felt tight, as if her skin had shrunk three sizes.

Her muscles contracted when his fingernail scraped the bottom edge of her curls. She whimpered and closed her eyes. A woman could only handle so much stimulation, and his hands on her skin promised an overload.

Cort lowered her leg and started all over again with her left leg. Deep massage. Featherlight brushes. Sheer heaven. Was it possible to drown in sensation? Her senses swirled. Her blood raced though her veins. An invisible corset squeezed her chest making it difficult to get enough air.

He reached the curls at the top of her leg, but skimmed over them to wash her belly. His hot, slick hands charged upward, causing her abdominal muscles to contract involuntarily. She had no idea the underside of her breasts could be so unbelievably sensitive. Her nipples tightened in anticipation of his touch, but he kept her waiting for several heart-pounding seconds.

"Tracy, look at me."

She forced open her heavy lids. He rewarded her by cupping her breasts and flicking his thumbnails over the beaded tips. Her bones melted and she cried out.

"A perfect fit. Good?"

He had no idea how good. If he hadn't been holding her up she would have slid under the water. Her head lolled back on the curved rim of the tub and her lids drifted closed. "Yes."

A hot blast of breath on her cheek was the only warning she had before his mouth covered hers in a kiss hotter, wetter and wilder than anything she'd ever fantasized about under the cover of night. Their tongues twined and tangled, stroked and teased, chased and retreated.

She shoved her wet hands through his hair and held on. She could become addicted to his kisses.

Cort rolled her tight nipples between his thumbs and forefingers. She moaned into his mouth and arched into his touch. Bliss. He nipped her lips and one of his hands stroked downward not stopping until he'd reached the focal point of need between her legs. He'd brought her pleasure with his touch before, but her body hadn't been as primed then as now. The deft stroke of his fingers was too much and not enough at the same time.

She parted her knees, and he slipped a finger inside her. Her internal muscles clenched him. She didn't mean to make it happen. It just did and...*oh, my*. Pleasure vibrated along her nerve endings. She squeezed again and sensation rippled through her. He stroked her until she whimpered.

"Easy," he murmured against her lips while still creating magic with his hands.

Nothing could have prepared her for the intimacy of having a part of him inside her or the intense yearning that made her shamelessly lift her hips and open her legs farther. A second finger joined the first, and his thumb brushed over her center, sending fire licking through her veins. The combination of his mouth and hands fueled the spark until she burst into flames.

His kiss gentled. He lifted his head. She couldn't imagine a more potent aphrodisiac than the hunger in his eyes or the tension straining his features.

Cort wanted her. *Her.* The high school brainiac. The kid from the wrong side of the landfill.

"Time to rinse off." He stood, pulling her with him.

Her legs quivered and threatened collapse while he adjusted the water. Water pulsed over her from the showerhead until he shut it off abruptly, whisked a towel around her and swept her off her feet. He carried her to her darkened bedroom, and she clung to his shoulders as her senses spun. Her body slid against his as he set her on her feet beside her high four-poster bed.

He ripped back the covers, pulled the clip from her hair and clicked on the bedside lamp. A rosy glow filled the room. His gaze took in her canopied, lace-draped bed. "Girly."

"I'm a girl."

"Yeah." He managed to squeeze several syllables

into the short word, making it sound more like a growl than speech. The wicked promise in his eyes sent her heart racing even faster, but when he whipped his shirt over his head, the pounding organ shuddered to a stop before stumbling back into an uneven rhythm.

Her palms grew damp. In the bathtub she hadn't worried about her role in this escapade because it had been pretty obvious she was the one being bathed. Now she worried. What was she supposed to do next? Hesitantly she laid a hand on the warm skin of his chest. His heart pounded beneath her palm.

Cort hooked a finger in her knotted towel, and it dropped to the floor. Before she could cover herself he captured her face in both hands and kissed her. Hard. Deep. Ravenously. As if he wouldn't survive for another minute if he didn't consume her.

Her simmering desires boiled over and her nervousness eased. She trusted Cort, and she craved the experience of loving him. She tugged at his belt, but her fingers fumbled at the unfamiliar task. He drew back slightly to help, and then his pants and briefs hit the floor.

She barely caught a glimpse of his thick shaft before his arms banded around her, pulling her flush against the hot, hard length of his body. Bare skin to bare skin he sealed her lips with his and captured her needy sounds with his mouth. The wiry hairs on his chest teased her breasts, and his erection seared her belly. One thick thigh pressed between hers, touching off a bonfire of need.

She gasped, pulling the air from his lungs and into hers. She needed to touch him—all of him. Twining her arms around him, she glided her hands over his lower back and tight buttocks.

He dug his hands into her waist and forced a few inches between them. "Whoa. Slow down, Trace."

"I can't." Hot skin. Male scent. Sensory overload. Her fingertips grazed the tops of his thighs, and the crinkly hairs tickled her palms.

"Then, darling, we're in trouble because I'm not sure I can, either. Sure you want to do this?" His eyes searched hers.

"Absolutely." The strength of the hunger swelling within her surprised and overwhelmed her.

He backed her toward the bed, and she sat on the edge of the high mattress. Cort stepped between her open knees and bent to capture her nipple with his hot mouth.

Desire twined through her like the morning glory vine spreading over her back fence. She dug her fingers into the supple skin on his shoulders and arched her back.

With a hissing breath, Cort pulled back. He snatched up the box of condoms, ripped it to get what he needed and then dropped the box. He carried a plastic package to his mouth in an unsteady hand and tore it open with his teeth.

Tracy swallowed hard and opened her palm. A mature woman handled this part for her man, for *herself*. She'd practiced the proper usage of a condom on a banana just like every other kid in health class, but a soft, cool banana had little in common with the hot, hard, pulsating man in her hands. She fumbled. His hand covered hers, demonstrating the correct technique, and together they stroked the thin latex over his thick shaft.

Her exploration ventured lower to his soft silky skin, his muscular thighs.

"Stop." He ground out the word through clenched teeth and locked his hands around her wrists.

Had she done something wrong? She jerked her gaze to his face, but his eyes were tightly closed, his teeth bared as he sucked in air. The tendons of his neck stood out.

He laced his fingers through hers and devoured her mouth, easing her backward one vertebra at a time until the cool sheets cradled her hot skin, and their clasped hands bracketed her head. His thick shaft pressed against her moist entrance and withdrew, priming her until she shifted eagerly, silently begging him to assuage the tension building in her belly.

He penetrated an inch—*two*—and groaned against her neck. She wanted more—wanted him so badly that every muscle in her body contracted in anticipation. Planting her feet on the side rail of the bed, she lifted her hips to take him deeper. He swore and drew back.

"Look at me, Trace." His hungry gaze pinned her to the mattress as surely as his body did. "Breathe," he ground out.

She hadn't realized she was holding her breath until he said so, and when she inhaled, the hot, musky aroma of arousal made her dizzy. She tightened her fingers on his.

The desire in his eyes would feed a lifetime of fantasies. "Now exhale."

When she did he thrust through the barrier of her innocence, burying himself in one long, smooth stroke. The brief flash of pain surprised her but quickly subsided.

His chest heaved against hers. "Breathe, Trace."

"I…can't," she wheezed. He'd filled her so full there wasn't any room for anything else—not even air.

"Hurt?"

Hurt? Oh, no. She forced her heavy lids open, looked into his eyes and smiled. "No. Amazing."

"Don't look at me like that or I'll lose it."

She smiled at his absurd comment. She'd never been the kind of woman to drive a man wild with just a glance. But with Cort, she felt as if it might be possible.

The rightness of being this close to Cort, of having him inside her, surrounding her, overwhelmed her, and her eyes burned. She didn't want to cry and make a fool of herself, so she pulled her hands free and wrapped her arms around his middle. Arching up, she tasted the salty skin of his neck and kissed the slight stubble on his tense jaw.

With a groan he banded his arms around her and straightened, pulling her into a sitting position. He wrapped her legs around his waist as he stood beside the bed. Tangling his fingers in her hair, he kissed her slowly, deeply, loving her mouth with a restrained hunger that left her breathless. He stroked her face, her neck and her breasts, searing a path everywhere he touched.

Mirroring his movements, she glided her fingertips over his sweat-dampened skin and tasted his shoulder, his flat nipples and the pulse pounding at the base of his throat. She traced the gold chain holding his St. Christopher medallion with her tongue.

He whispered her name in an agonized plea, cupped her bottom, and held her steady as he withdrew only to plunge inside her again and again. Each thrust went deeper, forcing the air from her lungs and making her heart race faster. Tension coiled tighter and tighter inside her, and then he touched her. One brush of his finger and she shattered into a million fragments.

Cort's muscles knotted beneath her fingertips, and

then he threw back his head and groaned. She held him close and buried her face in his neck, inhaling his scent and tasting his sweat on her lips as he shuddered in her arms.

Emotion clogged her throat. She feared she'd given more than her body to Cort tonight, and she said a silent prayer that he wouldn't break her heart this time.

He'd died and gone to heaven. Cort's arms and legs trembled, threatening to give out.

"Cort."

Tracy's breathless whisper fanned the embers inside him, and if she moved like that one more time, she was going to get more loving than a virgin ought to get on her first time out of the gate. His protective instincts kicked in.

Don't be greedy, Lander.

He pressed her back onto the mattress and groaned into her ear when she pressed an openmouthed kiss against his shoulder. Her teeth grazed his skin and he shivered. He eased back a smidgen. His depleted muscles refused to carry him any farther.

She opened her eyes and something deep in his gut knotted. Tears? Regrets? He hoped not.

And then she smiled and his tension unraveled. He'd never felt closer to anyone. Not even Kate. A warning prickle crept down his spine. He'd loved Kate, hadn't he? But if he'd loved her, then why hadn't he felt the sense of rightness he experienced here and now with Tracy?

She stroked his cheek and then his lips with her finger. "Thank you."

The warmth spreading through the pit of his stomach warned him that making love with Tracy would change things. Forever. "'You're welcome' hardly seems appropriate."

Her lips curved upward, but this wasn't her usual reserved smile. This one was so damned sexy and womanly his knees buckled and banged against the side rail before he could catch himself. Pain radiated from his bruised kneecaps, but then she moved beneath him, stretching like a sated cat, and fire of a different sort replaced the pain. She curled her legs behind his thighs, pressing his butt with her heels and seating him even deeper inside her. Oh man, the woman was hell on his willpower.

"Are you being greedy, Trace?" The gravelly rough voice didn't sound like his.

"No." She nibbled her swollen bottom lip. "Yes. But I understand if you need recovery time."

His ego—along with a certain part of his anatomy—swelled.

He withdrew from her body, grabbed a tissue and dealt with the condom. Lifting her into the center of the bed, he stretched out beside her and did his best to kiss the living daylights out of her and show her how appreciative he was of the gift she'd given him. Judging by the nails digging into his spine and the sighs she breathed into his mouth, he wasn't doing a half-bad job, but Tracy gave as good as she got and she wasn't the only one gasping when he lifted his head.

Her silky skin brushed him from ankle to lips, and she wouldn't lie still, so every one of her inches tormented every one of his. He wanted to explore all of her, but he'd planned to take it easy tonight. Tracy obviously had other ideas.

He grinned against her breasts—Tracy had the most sensitive breasts—and captured one stiff peak in his mouth. She whimpered and he suckled harder. Her fingers tangled in his hair, holding him close as he laved her.

He ventured down her midline to her navel, drawing closer to the heady scent of her arousal until he finally found his pot of gold.

She sat up abruptly. Her eyes rounded. "Cort, I don't think—"

"Easy. Relax." He nudged her back with a knuckle on her breastbone. "If you don't like me kissing you here I'll stop, but give it a thirty-second try first. Trust me?"

She chewed her lip and then nodded.

He kissed her lips and stroked her silky skin until her tensed muscles loosened. When she became pliant in his arms he worked his way down her body, nibbling and sipping. With the first stroke of his tongue on her soft feminine flesh her hands fisted in the sheets beside her hips until her knuckles turned white. The cadence of her breathing quickened as he led her closer and closer to release, and then she cried out as a climax racked her body.

The sounds she tried and failed to stifle behind her fist turned him on like never before. He wanted her again. He shouldn't. She wiggled against him, and suddenly he didn't give a rat's behind about what he shouldn't do.

Tracy had always pushed him to be the best. Tonight he intended to show her just how good he could be.

Grabbing a condom, he eased into her damp heat and carried them both to paradise.

Seven

Tracy's pulse accelerated as she reached the kitchen. Her shortness of breath had little to do with her sprint down the stairs and everything to do with the man waiting to heat her up.

She paused in the doorway to wipe her damp palms on her skirt. The last two days as Cort's lover had been...phenomenal. He'd been an unbelievably tender tutor and amazingly insatiable.

She wrinkled her nose and grinned. Apparently, insatiability was contagious.

Cort looked up from the medical textbook in front of him on the table. "Josh asleep?"

"Yes." She practically panted the word. She'd grown up surrounded by men in chambray and denim. Was that why khaki and interlock knit made her mouth water?

Without taking his eyes from her, he closed the book

and shoved it aside. His expression didn't change, but the heat in his gaze increased about six hundred degrees, making her skin tingle and flush. With just a look he made her feel like the sexiest woman on the planet. "How long do we have?"

Her nipples tightened and her blouse clung to her sensitive breasts. She plucked at the fabric, inching the hem from her waistband for ventilation, and then wet her dry lips. "He usually naps an hour or two, but he may sleep longer today since I exhausted him at the park this morning."

A wicked smile kicked up one corner of his mouth as he stood. "The clock's ticking. Your bed or mine?"

Never in her life had she spent a Saturday afternoon in bed, not even when she'd been ill, but she had every intention of doing so today. Her hormones had been in an uproar since Cort winked at her over his omelet this morning and reminded her that the clinic closed at noon on Saturday. He'd asked her not to make plans for nap time.

How could she tell him she didn't think she could wait until they reached the bedroom? Closing the distance between them, she wound her arms around his middle and tipped back her head. Always a quick study, Cort didn't need additional prompting to kiss her until her thoughts addled.

He tasted of sweet tea and hungry male—an addictive combination. She feared she would suffer withdrawal symptoms when he left at the end of the summer, but she didn't want to think about that now, not with his hands skimming over her and setting her skin ablaze with need.

Like a mime, she mirrored his actions, pulling his shirt from his waistband and tunneling her fingers beneath the hem to knead his back. Muscles bunched and flexed under his supple, warm skin. Impatient, she shoved at the fabric impeding her explorations until he whipped his polo shirt over his head and tossed it over his shoulder. She dipped to sample the salty tang of his hot flesh with her tongue and inhaled deeply. His unique scent mingled with that of his cologne to fill her senses and make her head spin.

Cort tangled his fingers in her hair, threw back his head and groaned as she licked her way from his chest to his collarbone. "We won't need the entire hour if you keep that up, Trace. Hell, we won't need five minutes."

A thrill raced through her. Knowing she could arouse him increased her own confidence and desire tenfold. She nipped at his skin, and he shuddered. Evidently, the love bite aroused him as much as it did her because he lifted her to sit on the table, stepped between her knees and went to work on the buttons of her blouse.

She had an inkling her kitchen table was about to be used for a purpose for which it was never intended. Naughty excitement percolated through her bloodstream.

He shoved open her shirt. Cool air swept her burning skin seconds before his hot mouth erased any cooling effect the ceiling fan might have generated. Gently kneading her aching breasts, he nibbled a path from her neck to her collarbone before tracing the outline of her lacy bra with his tongue. She arched her back to give him better access, and he complied by taking her into his mouth, lace and all.

She gasped and moaned, dragging her fingers from his short hair to his wide shoulders as intense pleasure spun and swirled in her belly. Cort reached for the tie of her wraparound skirt and at the same time she un-hooked his belt. She wanted and needed him with an urgency she'd never experienced before—an urgency that bordered on the verge of being out of control. Each time they made love she dared to be a little bolder. Releasing his zipper, she tunneled her fingers beneath the fabric and cupped her palm over the thick ridge of his arousal, stroking his satiny shaft until he groaned against her breast.

The rusty screech of her back door doused her desire like a waterfall on a lit match. Cort went rigid and straightened. Her eyes flew open, and she yanked her hand out of his pants. She looked over his bare shoulder and her heart stopped.

Wearing matching shocked expressions, Libby and Chuck stared at them from the threshold.

Tracy snatched the sides of her shirt together. She couldn't stand or her untied skirt would fall at her feet. Cort yanked up his zipper and turned in front of her, even though anyone could plainly see his bare chest and the distention of his khakis beneath an unbuckled belt. It wouldn't take a coach's playbook to know the score.

Panic and embarrassment sent another chilling wave crashing over her body, but even though she'd rather hide behind Cort's broad shoulders, she'd never been one to shirk blame.

A heavy silence filled the kitchen while she fumbled to button her shirt with fingers that refused to cooperate. Dear Lord, if anybody had to catch them in the act, why Libby and Chuck? Those two had more connections and talked more than anyone in the entire county.

"Tracy, are you okay?" Libby's quiet voice sounded like a fire alarm in the silent kitchen.

Over Cort's shoulder she saw Chuck push the door the rest of the way open. He entered the kitchen like a gladiator ready to do battle. "Do I need to talk to him?"

Chuck's tone implied he'd "talk" to Cort with his fists, even though one arm bore a cast from armpit to fingertips.

"No." Clutching the ties of her skirt, Tracy slid off the table and stepped out from behind Cort.

Chuck glowered. The red of his face made the white tape over his stitches stand out. "He's taking advantage of you."

"No," she repeated. Her dream of being principal of County ebbed out of her grasp. A woman willing to have an illicit affair would be deemed unsuitable to guide children.

Cort gripped her elbow and turned her, pinning her with a hard stare. "Tracy, don't—"

She wouldn't let Cort pay for her mistake. "Cort and I… Our relationship is…"

"He seduced you." Chuck might have quit playing football years ago, but he still worked out with his players and every one of his bulky muscles flexed.

Oh, God, why couldn't the floor open up and swallow her? Her fingers trembled when she knotted the ties of her skirt. She inhaled and exhaled slowly. "No. I prop—"

Cort grasped her shoulders and spun her to face him. "Trace, why don't you let me handle this?"

He tried to telegraph a message with his eyes, but her rattled nerves couldn't pick it up. Resignation tightened his features. He laced his fingers through hers and touched his lips to her forehead. She stiffened in surprise.

"Tracy and I wanted to keep our secret a little longer,

but I can see that's not going to be possible." Cort roped his arms around her shoulders and pulled her close, but his muscles were as tense as her own. "I've asked Tracy to marry me, and she's accepted. We were celebrating when you came in. You can keep the celebrating part to yourselves, can't you?"

Her stomach dropped to her feet and her heart raced. Was he serious? Of course he wasn't. In a few weeks he'd return to school and she'd stay here. Cort had fabricated this engagement to salvage her reputation.

"Cort—"

A sharp stabbing glance warned her not to correct him. "I'm sorry, darlin', but I'll bet we can count on Libby and Chuck to keep our secret. They know how it feels to be in our shoes." He dropped back into the Texas drawl she hadn't heard from him since he'd left for college.

She blinked. Keep secrets? Libby and Chuck? Was he out of his mind? No, he wasn't. Libby's mother was on the school board, and Chuck's father was a deacon at the church. Cort knew that if Libby and Chuck talked, in a matter of hours the community would be buzzing with news of their engagement or their entanglement, if she refuted his claim. She wanted to kiss him for trying to protect her.

He faced their guests. "We haven't told our families. Could you give us a few days to make plans?"

Her family. Her knees wobbled. What would she tell her parents? How could she explain her affair or the pretend engagement? Hadn't her parents been disappointed and embarrassed enough by their children's stupid choices?

Libby inched forward. "Is this for real?"

Should she continue this farce? Did she have a

choice, if she wanted to keep her name in the running for the job? Tracy managed a nod because there was no way she could force a lie past the lump in her throat.

Libby squealed and launched herself at them. She hugged Tracy, Cort and then Tracy again.

Tracy didn't know what to say. Guilt racked her for lying to Libby. She couldn't pretend an excitement she didn't feel. On the other hand, if the engagement were real… No, she didn't mean that. Her life was here, and Cort's was halfway across the country. He dreamed of a big-city practice, and her pride demanded that she stay here and prove her worth.

"I just knew it when I saw the two of you together at the dance." And then Libby sobered. "Wait, does this mean that you convinced him to stay or that he's taking you away from the job that means the world to you?"

Beside her Cort stiffened and she glanced at him in near panic. Did he have any idea about the backlash from this lie? If he stuck by his plan to return to medical school, the board would remove her from the list of applicants.

"I…I…" She had no idea what to say.

Cort's gaze held hers. "If Tracy gets the job, then we'll stay."

Her knotted muscles clenched tighter, the old cliché about weaving a tangled web couldn't have been more apt. Any minute now a big hairy spider was going to come and bite them on the—

"So when's the wedding?" Libby asked.

A hot brick settled in Tracy's stomach. Lies. She'd always prided herself on honesty.

Cort held up his hand. "We don't have any details yet."

Libby quizzed, "You'll let me know as soon as you do?"

Again Cort answered when Tracy couldn't have said a word if her life depended on it. "Yes. Now what brought the two of you here this afternoon?"

Chuck, his expression slightly less pugilistic, cleared his throat. "I wanted to thank you for looking out for me and my team after the accident. You're a real hero, Lander. Kept your cool and executed your duty. I was sure glad to have you on my side, man."

Looking as if the praise made him uncomfortable, Cort shifted on his feet and shook Chuck's hand—the hand that had been willing to pound him just moments ago. "You're welcome."

"Anything I can do for you, you just holler, you hear?"

"Thanks."

Chuck cleared his throat. He grabbed Libby's elbow and dragged her toward the door. "Guess we'll let you back to your celebration, but this time, lock up. You know nobody knocks 'round here."

"Call me." Libby waggled her fingers.

The door closed behind them, and silence filled the kitchen. Tracy pressed her fingers to the headache forming behind her temples and faced Cort. "Cort, you shouldn't have."

"Come here."

Her pulse skipped a few beats, but she needed to focus on the horror of the snowballing disaster ahead, not the desire Cort could kindle with just a look. Heavens, what a mess they'd made of things. "I don't think now is the time to—"

He shook his head. "You're buttoned wrong."

With a gasp she looked down at her blouse. She'd

misaligned the buttons. Embarrassment scorched her cheeks. She hastily corrected the problem. "Why did you make up that story?"

"Can you think of a better option? The folks around here will accept a little sparking between an engaged couple, but two singles having wild sex under the same roof as a minor is guaranteed to ruin any chance you have of getting that job."

He couldn't have been more right, but she couldn't overlook the impending disaster. "But—"

He held up a hand. "You can dump me right before Josh and I head back for Durham. In the meantime we need to follow this through."

"But Doc Finney is going to believe he has a permanent replacement, and he's going to put his retirement plans into motion. You can't disappoint him at the last minute."

Cort swore and shoved a hand through his hair. "Give me another option."

If only she could. "I don't have one. We'll tell our families the truth, won't we?"

He stayed silent for a moment. "I wouldn't recommend it. If they're not talking about or planning a wedding, folks will figure it out. Your job and your reputation are at stake, Trace."

"I know." She chewed her lip. What kind of school and community leader would she be with questionable integrity? And how would her parents handle another disappointing child? "We're lying to everybody?"

"Everybody but ourselves."

"You're kidding me." Cort grabbed Tracy's hand as she slid out of his bed. Her bare skin, mussed hair and swollen lips stirred a fire in his belly even though it had only been minutes since he'd satisfied his hunger for her.

Tracy reached for her robe with her free hand. "I go to church every Sunday, and after your announcement yesterday, I don't dare skip a day or folks will know exactly what we're doing."

He sat up in bed, all traces of warmth and contentment doused. The walls of this stuffy community closed in on him. "I haven't been to church since Brand got married."

"You don't have to go." She tugged her hand free and tied her robe.

"You want me there?"

For a minute he didn't think she'd answer and then she sighed. "It would be easier than explaining why you're not."

He shoved back the covers and stood, taking satisfaction in the way her breath hitched, and her gaze devoured him. He liked it even better when her eyes widened at his obvious response and she licked her lips. "I don't suppose the hot topic will be the preacher's sermon."

"No." A flush tinted her cheeks and she averted her gaze. "I love Libby, but she can't keep a secret to save her life, and the juicer it is the faster she talks. Chuck isn't much better."

Damn. "We'll be under the microscope?"

"Yes." Her paling skin indicated she didn't relish the idea any more than he did. He couldn't blame her. He'd rather spend a hot summer day cleaning stalls and swatting flies than a single hour under the scrutiny of her gossipy neighbors, but Tracy had always been there for him and he owed her.

What in the hell had he been thinking when he concocted that story? The problem was he hadn't been thinking. He'd taken one look at Tracy's ashen face, and he'd wanted to help. She gave unstintingly and never asked for anything in return. He knew for a fact that the money she earned from tutoring him had gone toward family bills. He'd offered the first solution that came to mind, but after ten years, he'd forgotten the reality of the gossip mill in this community. His good intentions had blown up in his face.

At least he still had her friendship, and together they would unravel the snarl he'd made even if it took the rest of the summer to do it. "Shower together?"

She gave him a teacher's under-the-brow look that made him think of playing hooky and afternoons in the hayloft. His pulse kicked up a notch. She knew as well as he did that if they showered together they'd miss the service. "I don't think so."

He grinned. "Spoilsport."

Instead of responding to his teasing, she twisted her fingers and worried her bottom lip with her teeth. "Cort? My parents will be at the service, and it's likely some of your family will, too. We should have called them last night."

Damn. He'd hoped to find another way to clean up this mess—one that didn't require lying to family and Doc Finney. In the past he'd always been able to come up with a plan B or C when plan A failed, but no such luck last night. Of course, instead of lying awake thinking of a solution, he'd reached for Tracy, and rational thought hadn't been a priority. "I wanted to work the kinks out of our story first."

"There's no way to a perfect lie."

"No." When the time came for him to return to North Carolina he'd have to take the fall for their breakup so folks wouldn't blame Tracy, but he'd have to be careful. If he painted himself as too much of a bastard, his family would feel the backlash of the gossip.

Josh announced his wakefulness in the other room. "If we take turns with Josh we should both be able to shower and get to the church on time."

"You don't have to—"

He laid a finger on her soft lips. "We're in this together, Trace. No matter what, I'll stand beside you. Now, hit the shower or I will be in there to hurry you along."

The service had started by the time Tracy and Cort got Josh settled in the church nursery and slipped into the back pew.

She knew the exact moment they'd been spotted by the way heads turned in the congregation. She couldn't hear the whispers, but she could see the furtive glances, the tilted heads and the moving lips as word spread—a chilling reminder of the times when her sister's and brother's scandals had rippled through the community grapevine. Any hope that Libby had kept her secret died.

Cort clasped her cold hand in his and rested their joined hands on his thigh. Whether he did so in support or as part of the charade, she didn't know, but she welcomed his warmth. Her hands were cold. She feigned interest in the program she held in her trembling fingers and surreptitiously scanned the church.

Her parents were there in the third row, the same as always. Cort's father and stepmother were on the opposite side of the church. They should have called them last night and explained the situation, but she'd hoped to come up with another solution by morning—one that wouldn't shame her parents or cost her the principal job. She hadn't.

Taking Cort as a lover had been a mistake—not just because of her reputation, but because selfish deeds never went unpunished. She'd wanted closure on her past crush, but instead, Cort and his son took another piece of her heart each day. If she had any common sense at all she'd tell him she wanted to go back to being landlord and nanny before she lost herself to the Lander man completely.

How could she when it would be an absolute lie? One lie was enough.

The congregation stood to sing and Cort's arm encircled her waist. Startled, she looked up at him and bit her lip. His gaze dropped to her mouth, and the understanding in his eyes transformed into something hot and sultry and not at all appropriate for a sanctuary. His grip tightened on her hip. Her breath caught and her skin flushed.

Dear Lord, please don't let this be the biggest mistake of my life.

The service lasted an eon. She got through it by concentrating on Cort's pleasant baritone when he sang the hymns. She had a panicky moment when the pastor called for members of the congregation to stand and ask for prayer for those who were ill, traveling, expecting or any number of other reasons. She could have sworn the pastor looked directly at her when he asked if anyone else needed a blessing. She managed not to squirm, but the hard wooden pew became decidedly uncomfortable.

Finally the service ended. Outside the church the summer sun beat down, making her dress cling to the skin between her shoulder blades. The scent from the church rose garden hung heavily in the air.

Cort led her to the shade of the huge pecan tree on the front lawn. "I don't suppose we can cut and run, now that we've put in an appearance?"

She wanted to bolt, but that would be too easy, too telling. "No, we have to talk to our families as well as face anyone else who has something to say."

Most of the congregation headed straight for the air-conditioned parish hall for refreshments. Her parents exited the church right alongside Cort's father and stepmother. Every muscle in Tracy's body tensed when her mother spotted them and hurried in their direction. The Landers followed, and the two couples stopped in front of them, the women with expectant expressions, the men with guarded ones.

Her father looked the most suspicious. "Is there something you need to tell me, son?"

Cort's fingers tightened on hers. "I've asked Tracy to marry me, sir. She's accepted."

Her mother launched at her, wrapping Tracy in a bouncing, excited hug. Tears rimmed her mother's eyes when she pulled back. "You knew what you wanted and you waited. You have always been my most persistent child—"

Alarm skittered down Tracy's spine. Her mother knew about her high school crush, and she didn't want that humiliating secret revealed. "Mom—"

Undeterred, her mother went on. "Have you set a date?"

Tracy looked from her mother to Cort, silently beseeching him to get her out of this mess.

He draped an arm across her shoulders. "Thanksgiving or Christmas. There's no need to rush into planning yet.''

He'd be long gone by then, and if her heart ached it was only because she knew that once he left she'd be pitied again. She found pity difficult to stomach.

''Then you're staying?'' Jack Lander's tone sounded hopeful.

A muscle in Cort's jaw ticked. ''If Tracy gets the principal job we'll consider it.''

Her mother beamed. ''She will. No one is more qualified than my Tracy. A wedding takes months to plan. We'll need to get started right away, Penny.'' She turned to Cort's stepmother.

''Mom—''

Penny interrupted, ''You'll need to book the church and the reception hall, Alice. And what about a ring? Have you bought a ring yet, Cort?''

''No, ma'am. There hasn't been time.''

Tracy wanted to cover her ears as the two women took off like the horses at the Retama Park racetrack plotting a wedding that would never happen, and when her father and Cort's started debating outdoor barbecues versus the church hall for the reception she wanted to scream. She looked away from their happy parents and her stomach sank.

Mrs. Blanchard picked her way across the lawn in their direction. The elderly lady never had a kind word to say to anyone. Some claimed she lavished so much love on her prizewinning roses that she had no tender feelings left for anyone else. ''Think your boy will marry this one before he gets her pregnant, Jack?''

Cort straightened beside her. ''I guess this means you haven't forgiven me for driving my truck through your rose garden fifteen years ago, Mrs. Blanchard. I apologized at the time, and I mowed your lawn for an entire summer.''

Jack Lander stepped forward. ''Don't you have anything better to do with your time than make folks miserable, Colleen?''

''I'd hate to see Tracy disgrace her momma and daddy the way David and Sherri have done. Your children have certainly been your cross to bear, Alice.'' The venomous light in the woman's eyes belied her sympathetic tone.

Cort's hand tightened on Tracy's, and when she dared to meet his gaze, she saw the questions he couldn't ask here and now. Shame crawled across her skin. He'd been gone for ten years and, evidently, he hadn't learned how much gossip the Sullivan family had generated during his absence. Once he did he'd be more than eager to end their pretend engagement.

Her mother bristled. ''We all make mistakes, Colleen, or didn't you listen to that sermon today? A more charitable person knows how to forgive and forget.''

''And a God-fearing man knows how to keep his pants zipped.'' Mrs. Blanchard flounced off.

Tracy's mother broke the heavy silence. ''Tracy, if we pick out the pattern and fabric this week I can start sewing your dress right away.''

The pastor's arrival prevented Tracy from having to reply. ''Glad to have you attending the service this morning, Cort. You and Tracy have chosen a beautiful day to announce an engagement.''

''Yes, sir.'' Cort's only sign of discomfort was the muscle ticking in his jaw.

''Seems right, the two of you together.''

Cort's steady gaze met and held hers. ''Tracy's always brought out the best in me, sir.''

The cold knot in her belly loosened. Cort would help her get through this.

"From where I stand, I see that it worked both ways. You pulled each other onward and upward from difficult circumstances to success. Your achievements are quite an inspiration for the younger members of our congregation."

Surprise flickered in Cort's eyes.

The pastor shook Cort's hand and patted his shoulder. "The flock is eager to welcome you home, son. Why don't we join the others in the parish hall so you can make your announcement? Let them share your joy."

A knife twisted in Tracy's heart. It was bad enough that she'd be hurt and embarrassed by Cort's departure, but her family and even the community would be, as well. She didn't see any way to prevent it.

How deep would this hole of lies get before it caved in on her?

Eight

"Turn here." Cort pointed to the dirt track leading down to the Nueces River and rolled down his window. The familiar scent of the river welcomed him, calmed him. The last hour had been tough. "I used to come here when I needed to be alone to think."

Tracy turned her sedan down the rutted track, guiding the vehicle through the overhanging branches. "I thought you brought girls here to make out."

He grinned at the flush tinting her cheeks. "A rumor intentionally started by me. A guy has to keep up his reputation. Besides, when did I have time? Between chores at the ranch, working at Doc's clinic, basketball practice and tutoring with you, I barely had time to brush my teeth. You're the first female I've brought here."

"You never brought Kate?"

"No. She wouldn't have appreciated the silence."

Her breath caught when she pulled into a clearing, and he couldn't blame her. Sunlight glinted off the slow-moving water with the brilliance of an operating room lamp. Insects buzzed. Fish splashed. His knotted muscles unwound. "The place hasn't changed much since the last time Doc brought me out here to fish and talk about medical school."

Climbing out of the car, he shucked his tie and suit coat before unbuckling Josh from the car seat. The crisp dried grass crunched under his feet as he strolled toward the riverbank. He glanced over his shoulder at Tracy. "Do you remember the day you caught me skinny-dipping here?"

"Yes." Her cheeks pinked.

"You ever try it?"

"No."

He grinned at her scandalized tone. "If we could get Josh to take a nap we could give it a go."

"I don't think so." The prissy way she stiffened contradicted the longing glance she cast toward the water.

He winked at her. "Just as well. I didn't bring protection, and I don't think I could see you all wet and naked and not want to be inside you."

She gaped at him and dampened her lips with the tip of her tongue. "Your ego is showing."

He'd often thought about that day during those first lonely years at Duke, wondering what she would have done if he'd climbed that riverbank, cupped her cheeks and kissed her right on her shocked, open mouth. Only their friendship and the fact that her brothers would have beaten the tarnation out of him had stopped him.

In McMullen County he'd been class valedictorian—a big fish in a small pond. At Duke he'd been just another fish in the school struggling to keep up. More than once he'd asked himself if he'd bitten off more than he could chew by leaving home, and if he wouldn't have been better off staying here and settling down with a local gal. He'd picked up the phone to call Tracy several times, but hung up before making a connection. She'd believed he had what it took to achieve his goal of being a doctor, and he hadn't wanted to let either her or himself down.

And then a few years later he'd met Kate. Kate had not only believed he had what it took to become a doctor, she'd pushed harder and suggested he had what it took to become a surgeon. He'd clung to her beliefs when he had doubts in himself. Kate, in a lot of ways, had taken Tracy's place in cheering him on when the workload became unbearable.

Before he'd left home he'd dreamed of buying this land from Doc and building a house here overlooking the river and Doc's favorite fishing spot. But somewhere along the line Kate's dream of living in a metropolitan area and having a posh office, a big house and fancy cars had taken precedence. He didn't remember when he'd changed course or why. Hell, fancy cars had never mattered to him. He still drove the old pickup he'd had back in high school.

Josh, none the worse for his hour in the church nursery, bounced happily in his arms and chanted, "Dadada."

He looked at his son's trusting smile, and his heart softened. Had it only been a week since he'd considered giving Josh up for adoption? Remembering the way Josh's features had lit up when he'd picked him up from the church nursery, he hugged him close. He had Tracy to thank for bridging the gap between them.

"I guess I've missed a few things while I've been

away. Care to clue me in to what David and Sherri have done that has Blanchard so fired up?''

Tracy chewed her lip and knotted her fingers. The sun picked out the fiery highlights in her hair and a light scattering of freckles on her nose. She had freckles in a few other places—places he'd touched and tasted. His heart hammered heavily and his groin stirred.

''David ran off with the science teacher's wife. They lived together for two years before Heidi's divorce came through. Sherri dropped out of school her senior year and left town with her boyfriend. She returned last year with one baby in her belly and another in her arms. She and the boyfriend never bothered to marry, and now she lives at home with my parents.''

Was this the sister Libby had said needed to get a life and a job? ''Old biddies like Blanchard live to throw it in your face. Why do you put up with the whispers, the stares and everybody butting into your business? Why do you stay, Trace?''

Her shoulders squared and her gaze held his. ''I stay because I want to prove that the Sullivan kids aren't white trash and that we will amount to something. Why are you so determined to leave?''

A gentle breeze plastered Tracy's dress against her curves. His blood heated predictably, but this wasn't the time or the place for what he needed. He turned back toward the water.

''I'll never be anybody but the youngest Lander boy here. I don't want to live my life in my brothers' shadows, and I've had enough meddling in my life from Caleb, Patrick and Brand. I don't need to add an entire community looking over my shoulder.''

The wind lifted strands of her hair, teasing it until she gathered it in one hand. ''I won't deny that folks around here are nosy. They condemn and chastise, but they're also right there when you need a hand. We're like family."

"I have a family."

She moved forward to stand beside him and touched his shoulder. "No, you don't, Cort. You've alienated yourself from them. You've only been home three times since your father's heart attack. I don't know what kept you away, but it was painful to watch you at the anniversary picnic and at the church reception hall today. You're standing on the outside and looking in."

Direct hit. He tensed up, and Josh started to fuss. Tracy held out her arms, and his son dove for her. She scooped him up and snuggled him close. Josh clasped her face in both hands and sucked her chin—his son's version of a kiss. He'd have to teach the kid a thing or two…in thirty years or so.

He shoved his hands in his pants pockets and paced along the bank. Rolling his reasons over in his head, he finally admitted, "I stayed away because Kate hated it here. She didn't like the ranch, and she wasn't crazy about my family."

Tracy inhaled sharply. "Why? You have a wonderful family, and Crooked Creek has turned into a real showplace."

"Kate had big dreams and the humble Lander household wasn't up to her standards. Even though Patrick had just inherited millions, we were still working class."

"She was a snob."

He'd never seen it that way, but Tracy was probably right. "She grew up poor, but she didn't plan to stay that way."

"So did I, but that doesn't mean I'll turn my back

on disadvantaged folks. My family is barely scraping by, in case you haven't noticed, and my parents still live in the same old house. The county may have covered over the landfill, but on a hot summer day if you're downwind, you can't miss that it's there. I'm not ashamed of my past, Cort. I'm proud of how far I've come when the odds were against me.'' She curled her fingers around his hand. ''You should be, too.''

He turned and studied Tracy. She'd grown stronger and more secure over the passing years. He couldn't help but respect and admire that. She looked at him over the top of Josh's head. ''If she didn't like who you were, then why did she choose you?''

Good question, one he'd bounced around often enough. ''I don't know the answer. Nor do I know why she dumped me.''

''Does it bother you more that you don't know why she loved you or that you don't know why she left you?''

Tracy knew him too well. She zeroed right in on his doubts. ''If I don't know what I did wrong with Kate, then how can I keep from repeating my mistakes?''

''Maybe the mistakes weren't yours. Maybe Kate was the one who needed work.''

Her answer surprised a chuckle out of him. Wrapping an arm around her waist, he pulled her forward to nuzzle a kiss against her temple. Her nearness and her scent stirred his senses. ''You always were my champion, Trace. Let's go home. We have twelve hours before either of us has to get up and go to work.''

Tracy yanked open the front door Monday evening before Cort reached her porch stairs. ''We have to *do* something.''

Her exasperated tone combined with her pale complexion and frayed braid warned him that her day might have been worse than his, and his had been challenging enough. The urge to pull her into his arms and slay her dragons startled him. The last thing he needed was to end up loving and losing Tracy the way he had Kate. He took the safer option and reached for Josh instead.

His son rushed into his arms—a first—and Cort's chest tightened. Josh planted one of his sucking kisses on his chin and squirmed closer, as if trying to burrow under his father's skin. He succeeded. This little boy he'd never intended to love had somehow wormed his way into his heart. He hugged his son close and looked at Tracy over Josh's soft, fuzzy head. His chest constricted even more. "What happened?"

Tracy paced the den, rubbing her temple and worrying her bottom lip with her teeth. She stopped, closed her eyes and heaved out a frustrated breath. "Your sisters-in-law came over today."

What was the problem? She liked Brooke, Leanna and Toni.

"They brought your nieces and nephews and *bridal magazines.*"

He winced. Patrick had shown up at the clinic and insisted on taking him to lunch. The main topic of conversation had been the wedding. His brother had not only offered to help pick out Tracy's ring, but to cover the costs of the ring and the whole damned wedding, for crying out loud. He'd be the first to admit that he'd never get rich off a resident's salary, but if he were going to buy Tracy a ring, he'd pay for it himself.

"Cort, your nieces begged to be flower girls, and your nephews want to be ring bearers. It was bad enough to lie to adults, but to disappoint the children…'' She resumed pacing the length of the room from fireplace to dining room. "I can't do this. I can't lie to everyone I care about just so that you and I can sleep together."

She stopped in front of him. "I want to go back to being just your nanny and landlord."

Whoa. "That's a little like locking the barn after the horses have been stolen."

"I don't care. I feel like a hypocrite. I'm asking the board to trust me with the most important position in the school, and I'm lying to them to get it. I can't do this," she repeated in a wobbly voice.

"You think you can ignore how good we are together?"

"I have to. I'll be your nanny during the hours we agreed upon, but I don't want to share meals or middle-of-the-night feedings anymore. Because of this lie we'll need to spend time together in public until you leave, but *only* in public."

The loss of Tracy in his bed bothered him, but not nearly as much as the wall she seemed determined to put up between them. He counted on Tracy's friendship, on her insights into the community and her help with Josh. Moving closer, he reached for her, but she stepped back, putting the coffee table between them.

Her fingers knotted until her knuckles turned white. "I'm losing my self-respect, Cort."

Her hoarse whisper put a lump in his throat. Nothing she said could possibly have hit him with more force.

Josh squirmed in his arms and Cort unlocked his tense muscles and set him on the floor. "There has to be an alternative."

"Sometimes you can't finesse your way around a problem. Did you talk to Doc Finney?"

Yet another difficult part of his day he'd rather not relive. "I told him that we were considering staying here, but that I wouldn't be comfortable in a practice on my own without a couple more years of training and supervision. That much is the truth."

"At least that will keep him from putting his home up for sale right away."

"You act like he's broadcasted his retirement plans."

"He has. Everyone knows that he wants to move to the beach and buy a boat, but he's been trapped here because he can't find a replacement willing to commit to practice in our rural area."

"What about his property by the river?"

"You'd have to ask him about that."

Doc had promised to sell him that land when he finished his training and returned home to practice. He couldn't hold Doc to that promise when he wasn't planning to stay here, but knowing that stretch of riverbank might soon belong to someone else didn't sit well.

"And now you get to meet Pam, sport," Tracy told Josh when she stopped at the clinic receptionist's desk.

Pam looked up from her computer screen. "Oh my, he's just as handsome as his daddy, isn't he?"

Pam's sly wink made Tracy squirm. "Yes. Cort called and asked me to bring Josh down for his nine-month checkup."

"Ricardo," Pam called to the teenager who worked part-time doing odd jobs in the clinic, "would you let Cort, I mean, Dr. Lander, know Tracy and Josh are here?"

"Sure. Hey, Miss Sullivan."

"Hello, Ricardo. How are you liking the job?" The teen was one of her brightest students, but he came from a disadvantaged family and needed all the breaks he could get.

"It's great. Doc's teaching me all kinds of neat stuff. Thanks for recommending me."

"You're welcome."

Ricardo disappeared down the hall.

Tracy carried Josh to the chairs and accepted congratulations on her engagement from the folks lingering in the waiting room. She was already cranky and irritable, but by the time Cort escorted Mrs. Klein past the front desk she was about to pull her hair out over the wedding questions. The lie had taken a life of its own, and every time she turned around it grew another tentacle.

Her gaze focused on Cort and her breath caught. She wasn't supposed to want him still, but her pulse increased and her mouth dried. He looked scrumptious. He'd traded his suit jacket for a white lab coat and removed his tie. The top two buttons of his light-blue shirt parted to reveal a few tufts of dark hair curling in the open collar, tempting her to tangle her fingers in the wiry curls. She clenched her fingers into a fist beneath Josh's bottom.

Cort spoke softly to the octogenarian and then escorted her out the front door. A welcoming smile replaced his troubled expression when he turned and spotted them. Josh reached for his daddy. Catching his son in his arms, Cort pressed a kiss to Josh's forehead and then leaned forward and brushed his mouth over hers.

"We have an audience," he whispered against her lips when she tried to pull away.

She cleared her throat and tried to ignore the way the bottom dropped out of her stomach.

Cort continued as if she weren't gaping at him like

a fish in a tank. "Thanks for bringing him down. Doc looked over Josh's medical records. When he realized that Josh is overdue for his immunizations, he offered to lead me through a well-baby exam."

"That's a good idea. The clinic treats a lot of children."

"Let me grab a chart from Pam, and we'll go back to a treatment room. We're on our own because the nurse left early today."

Tracy followed him down the hall and into a small room. Between the two of them they managed to strip Josh down to his diaper, but not without their hands and shoulders bumping. With each brush, Tracy's chest tightened and the air in the room thickened. Her olfactory system filtered out the medicinal clinic smell and homed in on the slight tang of Cort's cologne like a bee searching for pollen.

Why did doing the right thing have to be so difficult?

Cort went through the mechanics of weighing and measuring Josh and then listened to his heart and lungs. He looked in his ears and palpated his chubby tummy, much to Josh's delight.

Tracy had never seen Cort in action, but there was no denying his competence or his patience. When Josh balked, Cort teased him into acceptance. When Josh fussed Cort soothed him with a gentle touch. When he finished, he let Josh sit up on the exam table.

An awkward silence stretched between them while Josh gnawed on the tongue depressor. Glancing at his watch and then the door, Cort tucked his stethoscope into his lab coat and his hands into his pants pockets.

Concern darkened his eyes and pleated his forehead when he looked at her. "How have you been?"

It had been three long, silent days since they'd reverted to landlord and tenant. Other than the few words exchanged when Cort dropped off or picked up Josh, they hadn't spoken. "Fine."

His searching gaze ran over her as thoroughly as his hands had done previously, and her skin tingled. "Do you need anything? I saw the pain relievers on the kitchen counter this morning when I left Josh."

Her cheeks burned. She'd grown up having no secrets with four brothers in the house, but she'd never openly discussed her monthly cycle with any of them. "I'm fine."

His brow pleated. "Tracy—"

"I have cramps, all right." She couldn't believe she'd blurted that out.

Cort's lips pinched and his skin darkened. "Have you had them checked out to make sure everything is okay? I could—"

"*No.* I'm fine. Thank you." She didn't want to think of Cort examining her that way. Besides, if he touched her she'd probably beg him to come back to her bed despite the cramps. She missed him—not just his amazing lovemaking, but the conversations they'd had lying in the dark afterward. He'd told her about school and his roommates, and she'd lived vicariously through his stories. In return she'd filled him in on her siblings and students and their old friends. She missed him at breakfast and at dinner. She missed hearing about his day and the patients who puzzled him. She missed his touch, his scent, his taste.

Oh Lord, she was falling in love with him again.

"Sometimes birth control pills can reduce the discomfort during your period, and if medication doesn't work then there are the alternatives of using a heating pad or orgasm to relieve the cramping." He'd switched into doctor mode and he looked as relaxed and comfortable as she wasn't.

She couldn't believe they were having this conversation. "I don't have a heating pad, and I'm not interested in the other alternatives right now."

"Have you considered—"

"Cort, I have a physician and she's aware of the problem."

"She? You don't see Doc Finney?"

"No, I drive to Kingsville."

Silent, awkward seconds ticked past, and Cort's stomach knotted tighter with each one. He checked his watch again. What was keeping Doc? He'd been with his last patient when Tracy arrived.

Each time he looked at Tracy his chest hurt, so he played with Josh instead. He missed her. Worse, he thought about her throughout the day. Sometimes something a patient said would send his mind down the Tracy trail, and he'd have to ask them to repeat the entire conversation.

It was damned embarrassing to be so unprofessional, and it had never happened before. He'd loved Kate, hadn't he? But not once had thoughts of Kate intruded on his work. Disturbed by the realization, he reached for the doorknob. "I'll see what's keeping Doc."

He yanked the door open and found Doc standing on the other side. "Ready for me?"

"Yes."

Doc said hello to Tracy and went to work examining Josh. All the while he kept up a running dialog of what he was looking for and what he found. Cort took mental notes, but his retention of proper procedure very likely suffered because his antennae were tuned in to the circles under Tracy's eyes, the pallor of her skin, and the tight line of her mouth which told him more about her discomfort than she realized.

Doc finished his exam and pulled a vial and a syringe out of his pocket. "Healthy little boy. Now give him his immunization. Notice that I kept it in my pocket to warm it."

Tension pulled Cort's muscles. He'd given hundreds of injections before—but never to his own child. "I'm still bonding with Josh. Don't you think it would be better if you did it?"

"No, son, I don't." Doc's firm refusal didn't allow room for argument. He stood back with arms folded and watched.

Cort's hands trembled when he filled the syringe. It was just an immunization, for crying out loud. What kind of doctor would he be if he couldn't give a routine immunization? Gritting his teeth, he forced himself to go through the motions of cleaning Josh's thigh, of pinching up the skin and, finally, inserting the needle and dispensing the dose.

After a shocked second, Josh wailed, and everything in Cort snarled into an agonizing knot that only worsened when Josh reached for Tracy with fat tears rolling down his cheeks. Tracy scooped him up and held him tight while Cort stood by, shaking in his loafers.

He'd lost his detachment. Lost his professionalism. And the harder Josh cried the more nauseous he felt.

Doc laid a hand on his shoulder. "Lesson one, son. Fatherhood never gets easier. That little shot won't be half as bad as the first time you have to stitch his skin or the first broken bone you have to set for him. It'll happen. Prepare yourself. Won't be any different if it's Tracy you're working on. Sometimes love hurts, but there's nothing finer than caring for the ones you love."

Bile bubbled in Cort's throat at the thought of causing Josh more pain. He didn't want to consider hurting Tracy, but hurting her was inevitable. She'd pay the price of whispers and gossip when he left town.

"Dose him with pediatric pain reliever every four hours, as needed. Get yourself and the little tyke together, and I'll meet you at the front desk to sign off on your charts." Doc turned on his heel and left them, quietly closing the door on his way out.

Cort wiped an unsteady hand across his jaw and braced himself on the sink. He clutched the cool porcelain and took a fortifying breath. Hell.

Tracy touched his back. "Are you okay?"

"Fine." He washed and dried his hands, trying to collect himself before he faced her again.

When he turned and met her gaze, the understanding reflected in her eyes put a lump in his throat. Josh quit bawling, but his breath hitched in little gasps. Cort laid a hand on his warm back. "I'm sorry, son."

Josh dove for him, and Cort caught him and held him tight. His eyes burned. "I love him."

Tracy smiled, probably laughing at the wonder in his voice, but it was the first smile he'd seen from her in days, and it hit him like a sucker punch. "I know. It shows in everything you do for him."

"How? I've known about him less than three weeks."

She shrugged. "Love doesn't follow any rules. It just…happens."

He'd learned from Kate that love didn't just happen. It was damned hard work. "Let's get him dressed and get out of here."

Josh wouldn't let them put him back on the table. He bowed his back and protested, so Cort held him while

Tracy tugged on his clothes. Their hands tangled. Her breast burned against his bicep and her thigh against his. He couldn't help noticing that each time one of Josh's kicks connected with her belly she winced.

Mission accomplished, despite the fact that his fingers had turned into thumbs, he passed Josh back to Tracy and documented what he'd done in the chart.

He reached for the doorknob, but Tracy's hand on his arm stopped him. "Cort, you're a good doctor."

The sincerity in her eyes made him want to believe her, but he knew he'd just lost it. "I don't feel like one right now."

She stepped closer and wrapped one arm around him and the other around Josh and hugged them. "Caring is what makes you good at your job."

He cared about Tracy—probably more than was wise considering he'd be leaving in two months. Cort savored her softness and her cinnamon scent, not to mention her warmth and tenderness. His thoughts shifted from *being* a doctor to *playing* doctor with her, but he tamped down his response.

He opened the door and escorted her toward the front desk.

"Surprise!" The shout from the crowded waiting room made Tracy's heart lurch. Her family and Cort's, as well as Libby, Chuck and several other neighbors beamed at them.

Dear Lord, she wasn't up to this now. She pressed a hand to her lower abdomen.

While they'd been in the back with Josh, someone had transformed the room into an engagement party nightmare. White paper bells hung from the ceiling tiles. Balloons filled the corners of the room, and a refreshment table—complete with a cake and flowers—had been set up against the wall. Flashbulbs popped.

Cort pulled her close enough to whisper, "Smile for the camera, sweetheart."

She forced her lips into a smile and met his gaze. "You shouldn't have."

"I didn't. This is a surprise for me, too." No doubt her grin looked as phony as his.

One person after another passed her like a hot potato for hugs, kisses and best wishes. Her cramped stomach muscles protested every jolting move. She wanted to pick up her prescription, go home, curl up in bed and pull the covers over her head. How much worse could it get?

She wished she hadn't tempted fate when Cort's twin nieces stopped beside them. "Aunt Tracy, we found the perfect flower girl dresses."

Aunt Tracy? The girls acted as if the wedding was a done deal. Miranda held up a page torn from a magazine for her inspection. The girls' hearts would be broken and their feelings hurt because of this stupid lie. Tracy's stomach knotted and a tension headache boomed behind her left temple.

"It's a lovely dress, Miranda." Her voice sounded croaky, and her smile felt more like a grimace.

"Mom says if we could find one of those cute baby tuxedos then either Marissa or I could push Josh down the aisle in his stroller, and we could decorate the stroller with ribbons and flowers."

Tracy nodded like one of those bobble-headed dolls and tried to relax her jaw. If she clenched her teeth any tighter she'd need dental repairs.

Cort materialized beside her and pressed his hand to the small of her back as the congratulations from family and friends continued to rain down. How were they going to get out of this without hurting their families? With each moment that passed and with each person's good wishes her muscles cramped more and her head throbbed harder.

She was ready to scream by the time Libby stopped in front of them. Her friend's huge grin made Tracy want to cry in frustration. She'd lied, and dear Lord, she was paying for it.

She cleared her throat, prepared to confess even though it could hinder her selection as principal. She had no way of knowing exactly what Libby had told everyone, but it would be better to end this phony engagement now before folks spent more time and money on a wedding that would never happen.

"Libby, Cort and I got caught up in the reunion sentiment and rushed into this engagement. We—"

"Rushed!" Libby interrupted and then laughed. "Are you kidding me? You've been in love with Cort since eleventh grade. I'd say you're dragging your feet, girl."

Nine

The blood drained from Tracy's head, leaving her dizzy. Her ears burned with humiliation, and a chill seeped clear to her bones.

Cort laughed along with everyone else, but his laugh sounded forced, and his hand on her hip tightened. She could feel his gaze on her but didn't dare look at him, focusing instead on her knotted, white-knuckled fingers. Blowing out a slow breath, she tried and failed to come up with some witty way to deny Libby's remark.

Libby continued as if she hadn't just stripped Tracy's soul bare for the entire world to see. "So what do you say we have a summer wedding instead of a Christmas one, because I know you two can't wait to *celebrate* your love?" Libby waggled her brows and winked.

Tracy's stomach plunged to her feet. "I...I don't

think so. Cort and I need time to get to know each other again and to be sure this relationship is going to work.''

Libby leaned closer with a naughty glint in her eyes. ''Trust me, if the heat in your kitchen is any indication, your relationship will work just swell.''

Tracy's lips trembled. What could she say? What could she do except grit her teeth and get through this?

''Come and cut the cake,'' her mother called.

Glad for the escape, Tracy moved forward with stiff, jerky steps even though she'd rather run out the clinic door. Her sister Amy took Josh, and her mother swooped in dragging Cort. She posed the two of them with joined hands over the cake knife. By the time the amateur photographers were happy, Cort's groin was pressed snugly against her bottom. He hardened against her and her pulse rate tripled. She tried to shift away, but his hand on her hip held her still.

''Sweetheart,'' he whispered in her ear. ''If you have any mercy in your soul, hold still.''

Her head spun and her palms moistened. It would be a miracle if the knife didn't slip out of her grasp.

Together they carved right through the *congratulations* written in icing and slid the slice onto a plate. Duty served, she ducked out of Cort's embrace, praying for a moment alone, but he caught her hand and tugged her to a quiet corner.

''Trace, about what Libby said...''

Her humiliation intensified. She studied her shoes and then his left ear. ''I had a crush on you in high school, but girls outgrow crushes, Cort.''

His rigid shoulders relaxed. ''I didn't know.''

She risked a peek at his expression, but she didn't see ridicule in his eyes. ''I figured that out at the prom.''

"You want to explain to me what went wrong that night? We were having a good time and then you froze me out."

She averted her gaze, remembering the crushing blow to her pride. Her brother's basketball teammates had been laughing outside the men's room when she exited the ladies' room. They hadn't seen her, but she'd overheard their joking comments about Cort looking like he was having a good time even though everybody knew Tracy was a mercy date and that she wouldn't put out. She'd found and confronted her brother who'd admitted that he'd told Cort she didn't have a prom date.

She swallowed the lump in her throat and lifted her chin. "I didn't like discovering I was a pity date."

"A pity date?" She gave him points for the seemingly genuine surprise in his voice and expression.

"You only asked me because no one else had. Did David bribe you?"

"Hell, no. Trace, you must be the most generous person I've ever known. I volunteered because I wanted to repay you for all the help you'd given me. No girl should miss her senior prom."

She desperately wanted to believe him.

He cupped her jaw and tilted her chin with his thumb. "I miss you."

Her heart clenched. She chewed her lip. "I miss you, too."

"Can we have dinner together tonight?"

"No. Yes. Maybe." She shook her head and put a hand to the ache in her temple. "I haven't changed my mind, Cort. I can't live a lie just so that we can..."

"Rock each other's worlds?" He dipped his head and

brushed her lips with his. "Dinner, Trace, that's all I'm asking. We have to plot a way out of this mess."

"All right. Dinner, but that's it."

Dinner would be safe because they couldn't make love. Passion wouldn't cloud logic. They'd talk until they could find a way out of this engagement that wouldn't break their families' hearts, and then Cort would go upstairs *alone*.

Tracy shouldered open the kitchen door and set her grocery bags on the table. This whole pretend engagement debacle had her so worked up that she'd forgotten to pick up her prescription on the way home. She took an ibuprofen instead, hoping it would kick in before Cort and Josh arrived. No such luck. She grimaced when the front door opened and closed.

"Trace?"

"In here."

She heard him moving around in the den, and then he strolled into the kitchen with a bag from her favorite restaurant dangling from his fingers. The smell of barbecued chicken made her mouth water.

"I brought dinner, so you don't have to cook. Come on." He snagged her hand and dragged her toward the den. Josh played happily with his toys on the quilt in the corner. A new heating pad lay in the middle of her sofa. The glow of its little orange light told her it was already plugged in and turned on.

"Where did that come from?"

"I picked it up on the way home. Stretch out while I put supper together."

"I have to put away my groceries."

"I'll do it." When she didn't follow orders, he

cupped her chin in his warm hand. The genuine concern in his eyes melted her like butter in a hot pan. "I don't like to see you hurting."

Libby was right. She loved him and probably always had. The realization hit her like a two-by-four on the side of her head, winding her and making her dizzy. Before she could regain her equilibrium, he grabbed her shoulders and spun her toward the couch.

"Lie down on your belly. Position the heating pad where you're the most uncomfortable."

Numbly, she did as he asked and instantly the warmth seeped into her tight, achy abdomen.

"I'll be right back."

She loved Cort Lander. And he was going to leave her. Again. How would she survive it? She rested her forehead on her folded arm. How could she have let it happen? How could she have let Cort and his son into her heart? What a fool she'd been to believe that she could have a summer fling and kiss him and Josh good-bye without a second thought. Losing them would tear her to pieces.

Josh crawled over and pulled himself to standing beside the sofa. He leaned forward and gave her a sucking chin kiss. "Mamama."

Her heart nearly broke in two. She cupped his head and kissed his brow, trying to blink away the tears filling her eyes. She loved Cort and his adorable, motherless son. She'd honestly believed knowing that they'd leave at the end of the summer would prevent her from becoming attached, but it hadn't. She wiped a tear off her cheek and looked up to see Cort standing in the doorway.

She caught her breath at the solemn expression on his face. "He didn't mean—"

"It's okay, Trace. You're the closest thing he has to a mother right now. He's not going to remember Kate." He crossed the room, lifted Josh into his bouncy chair and sprinkled Cheerios onto his tray. After shrugging off his suit coat, he tossed it over the rocker and sat on the edge of the sofa. She tried to shift her legs to make room for him. "Don't move."

When she lay back down, he rolled up his sleeves and reached for the hem of her blouse. She stiffened.

"Relax. All I'm going to do is massage your lower back. I don't want to get oil on your clothes."

She hadn't noticed the small bottle of mineral oil on her coffee table until he picked it up. If she hadn't hurt so badly she would have refused. Instead she worked her shirt up to her bra strap and eased the elastic waist of her skirt down to her bikini panties. He poured a small amount of oil into his palm and then worked it into her skin, pressing and kneading her knotted muscles until she sighed in relief.

"Helping?" he asked without ceasing his hypnotic massage.

"Mmm." The combination of his firm, sure touch and the warmth created by the friction of the massage eased her discomfort and stirred a curl of desire in her belly. The love in her heart made her yearn for what could never be—Cort beside her forever as a husband and a lover.

"Willing to try the other alternative?"

"No." She tried to sit up, but he pressed her back into the cushions with his knuckles.

"I didn't mean intercourse. I meant I could pleasure

you like I did that first night to try and ease your pain. Let me know if you change your mind.''

He wiped the oil off her back with a paper towel and stood. ''Do you think your hardwood floors will withstand the demolition man if I bring his high chair in here, or should I feed him in the kitchen?''

She blinked. How could he go from offering to pleasure her to feeding Josh in seconds? Her brain struggled to catch up.

''The floors will survive.'' Knowing her time with them was limited, she wanted to soak up every second.

''I'll get dinner. You stay here and let the heating pad work its magic.''

As far as she was concerned he'd already worked all the magic she could handle for one night. What was she going to do? She had two choices. She could kick him out of her house and her life tonight and hurt now, or she could wait until he returned to North Carolina and hurt later. Neither choice appealed, but there were no alternatives.

Minutes later Cort had Josh in his high chair with an array of diced food. He disappeared back into the kitchen only to return and settle on the floor beside the sofa.

She frowned at the single plate with the food already cut into bite-size pieces. ''What are you doing?''

''I'm going to feed you.''

''I can feed myself.''

A dark brow arched. ''Lying down?''

''Well no, but—''

He shook his head. ''Lie back down. The only thing you need to do is lift your head and chew. I brought all your favorites.''

She hesitated.

"You know, Trace, for a woman who makes it her mission to take care of everybody else you sure make it difficult for anyone to return the favor."

Her heart squeezed tighter. Okay, so she had a slight problem with being beholden to anyone, but after years of hand-me-downs and charity, she had good reason to want to stand on her own two feet.

He took advantage of her inattention by tucking a morsel of chicken between her lips. A dab of barbecue sauce hung on the corner of her mouth. He swiped it with his finger and pressed it between her lips. The tangy sauce mingled with the flavor of Cort on her tongue and she swallowed hard.

He discarded the fork and used his fingers, feeding her a piece of corn bread and then popping the other half into his mouth. He did the same with the cinnamon apple wedges, the fried green tomatoes and the maple-glazed carrots. The latter was sticky and messy, and when he leaned forward to sip the maple syrup from her lips, her insides clenched into a tight, achy knot. He lingered, sipping and supping from her lips until she pushed him back.

"Cort—" Each of them was fully clothed, and Josh happily fed himself only a yard away, and yet the shared meal eaten from his fingers seemed intimate and sensual.

"Shh. You have to finish your dinner if you want dessert."

"How did you know my favorites?"

"The hostess is one of your students, and she helped me choose. I guess nosy neighbors have their uses." He fed her another morsel and then reached across to the rocking chair with his free hand and into his coat pocket. "Speaking of nosy neighbors, the pharmacist suggested you might need your prescription. Your symptoms must be severe to require this."

He passed her the bottle of cramp relief medicine. "Things have been a little crazy in the past few days, and I forgot to pick it up. It was kind of Mr. Wills to remember."

"Folks here look out for you."

"That's what I've been trying to tell you."

His gaze turned speculative before he stood and gathered the remnants of their meal. "Roll over and position the heating pad against your lower back. I'll get dessert."

He paused by Josh's chair. "Hey, buddy, you're making a killer mess."

Josh gave him a sloppy, food-laden smile, and Tracy's heart melted. These two had come so far in such a short time, and just as she'd expected, Cort made a great father. No matter what, she could never regret her role in bringing them together, nor could she regret her time with Cort.

Moments later Cort returned with a bowl, settled on the sofa beside her propped-up legs and spooned up a bite. "You like banana pudding?"

"Yes." Her mouth watered in anticipation, and her favorite dessert didn't disappoint. Tart and sweet and creamy all at the same time, she closed her eyes and sighed with pleasure. Cort's lips covered hers. Shocked, she swallowed quickly. He parted her lips and mated his tongue with hers in a slow, hypnotic dance. By the time he lifted his head she was breathless.

"Delicious." From the heat in his eyes, she didn't think he meant the pudding. He fed her another bite and took another kiss.

Her skin tingled and the cramps in her stomach turned into something else all together. "Cort, we can't."

He looked ready to argue, but then shrugged. For several heart-stopping seconds he studied her, and then a muscle ticked in his jaw. "Let's do it."

"Do what?"

"Get married."

She gulped and set her iced tea down on the end table before she splashed it all over herself. "What?"

"There's no way out of this engagement without hurting somebody's feelings, so marry me."

Pressing a hand to her chest, she tried to swallow the lump in her throat. "You don't love me, Cort."

He set the bowl on the coffee table and brushed his knuckle down her cheek. "But I trust you more than anybody I know, and I like you, Trace. We're good together."

"That's not enough."

"We could make it work. Come with me. There are dozens of schools near the Duke campus. You can get a job or just stay at home with Josh."

How many years had she secretly yearned for a proposal from this man? And now that she had one, she had to turn it down, but it wasn't easy. "Cort, I don't want to leave my family and my job to go to North Carolina with you, and you don't want to stay here."

"We can move back to Texas after I finish my training. I could start a practice in San Antonio."

"I can't." Proving herself and making her parents proud were too important. "My family needs me."

"What are you going to do when Josh and I leave?

When this fictitious engagement ends? Do you want to deal with the whispers and the stares? The pity?''

Anger and hurt battled for first place within her at the low blow. She straightened. Was this a pity proposal? ''I have to admit it would certainly be convenient if you didn't have to search for child care, but what about my plans?''

''You can apply for a principal position in North Carolina.''

''I need to do it here, Cort.''

He scrubbed a hand over his nape. ''We could be good together, Tracy.''

She respected herself to much to be any man's convenience. The most important thing she'd learned from her parents' thirty-year marriage was never to settle for less than true love. Her parents were a perfect example of how love could pull you through any hardship.

''If I ever marry it will be for love. I won't settle for less.''

His silence spoke volumes.

She piled her dishes on the tray and stood. ''Thanks for dinner. I think I'll try a hot bath and then go to bed. Good night.''

Even if Cort could have blocked Tracy from his thoughts at work over the next five days, his patients wouldn't let him.

They filled him in on his son and Tracy's daily activities, which was a blessing since each evening Tracy met him at the door with Josh, escorted them to the inside stairs and then firmly closed the door in his face.

He learned from one of the school board members

that Tracy should hear about the principal job by the end of the week.

He heard about Josh attending this child's birthday party or that child's swimming party. His son had been accepted into the community with open arms.

Evidently, he had, too. He learned more about his patients than he ever needed to know to make a diagnosis. Sure, they told him about their aches and pains, but they also told him about their nieces, nephews and cousins trice removed. They told him about their rose gardens, for crying out loud.

Worst of all, he'd become one of them. Mrs. Klein had nothing wrong with her as far as he and every test known to medical science could determine, except that she was eighty years old and lonely. He should have told her to get a pet, but instead he'd suggested she call up Mrs. Blanchard and show the old witch the new rose she'd just crossbred.

He'd meddled, dammit. Snapping her file closed, he shoved a hand through his hair and turned.

Doc watched him with a satisfied smirk on his face. "I wondered how long it would take you to figure out there was nothing wrong with her."

His ears burned. "I should have caught on quicker."

"If you'd asked Tracy you would have. She'd have told you that Callie lost her son last year and her husband two years before that. She just needs somebody to talk to. You were a new set of ears."

Cort ran a hand under the collar of his polo shirt and wished he'd worn his shirt and tie so he'd at least look less incompetent. "Right."

"Are you two going to be able to work this out?"

It shouldn't surprise him that Doc knew he and Tracy

were having problems, even though he hadn't mentioned the silence yawning between them to anyone. "I'm not sure."

"You still have your sights set on being a surgeon?"

Aware of the weight his answer carried, he chose his words carefully. "I haven't completely given up on that goal."

"Used to be your goals were a far sight different. Might be you need to backtrack and think on what changed your path. See you tomorrow, son. Believe I'll get me some fishing in before dark. You're welcome to join me, if you want. Same spot by the river."

"Tracy and Josh will be waiting."

Doc shook his head. "Third Tuesday of the month. All six of the Sullivan kids and their parents will be eating at Amy's house."

Tracy hadn't mentioned it. "Thanks, but I'd better head home."

Doc was right. The house was empty. Cort found a note telling him where Tracy and Josh were, right on top of a letter from Duke. He recognized his roommate's handwriting in the forwarding address scribbled on the envelope along with the word *Urgent*. His heart pounded and his mouth dried as he slipped his finger under the flap and tore it open. He read the letter once, twice and collapsed into the chair.

Dr. Gibbons had an unexpected opening on his team this term. If Cort wanted to accept it, he had to let them know immediately. Did he want the position? Hell, yes. Serving on Gibbons's team this rotation would put him a year ahead of his plans. But what about Josh? How long would it take Cort to find an apartment and child care he could afford? He couldn't dump his son just anywhere.

And Tracy? Would she reconsider going with him? The thought of leaving her behind opened a big gaping hole in his chest. If she wouldn't go, how would they end the engagement without causing her more pain and embarrassment?

He grabbed his keys and headed back out the door. He didn't have a clue where Tracy's sister lived, but chances were that anybody he stopped on the street could draw him a map. His theory proved true, and twenty minutes later he pulled up in front of Amy's tiny house.

Following the smell of grilling meat and the sound of voices, he cut a path to the backyard. Josh splashed in a shallow plastic wading pool with a couple of other kids. Tracy, reclining in a lawn chair right beside them, looked happy and relaxed until she looked up and spotted him at the gate.

She spoke to her sister, who sat in a chair on the opposite side of the pool and slowly rose to her feet. He almost swallowed his tongue. If he'd ever seen Tracy in a swimsuit, he didn't remember it. The black one-piece suit cupped and lifted her breasts, skimmed her narrow waist and made her legs look miles long. His heart beat faster with every bare footstep she took in his direction.

She stopped on the opposite side of the gate. "You found my note."

"Yes and I..." He couldn't find the words to tell her he was leaving—not at the end of the summer, but by the end of the week.

"And the letter from Duke, is it…important?" She pulled her bottom lip between her teeth.

"Dr. Gibbons has an opening on his team for the upcoming rotation."

Her chest quivered as she inhaled, and her hands gripping the gate turned white-knuckled. "Then you'll need to go back to Durham right away and get Josh settled."

"Yes." How hard could it be to say one word? "We can tell everybody that I'll come back at the end of the term, and then when you find somebody new—" A knot formed in his throat. He swallowed and took a deep breath. Tracy would find somebody new, and at the next ten-year reunion he'd come face-to-face with his replacement.

Deal with it, Lander. You knew this was temporary. But damn, it was harder to swallow than he'd anticipated.

He shoved a hand through his hair. "When you find somebody new, you can write me a Dear John letter to break the engagement. That should give folks less to talk about."

Tracy's solemn gaze held his. "We could tell the truth."

He winced. "Trace, don't. You know what would happen."

The angle of her chin rose proudly. "Yes, I do, but I'm twenty-eight years old, Cort. If folks want to fault me for trying to find happiness, then let them."

"Come with me."

The pain in her eyes made him want to pull her close. She gave him a watery smile and shook her head. "I can't. I owe it to myself to stay here and finish what I started.''

''Mamama,'' Josh called from the pool, and pain clouded her eyes.

''I have to get back to Josh.'' She opened the gate, took his hand and pulled him inside the fenced yard. ''Come and have dinner with us.''

He hesitated.

''Please.''

Cort let her lead him into her family knowing that this would be the last time they'd welcome him into their midst. As soon as the Sullivans learned the truth, they'd probably be gunning for him.

For the next two hours her family welcomed him and Josh as if they'd been a part of the Sullivan clan for years. God knows how many hours he'd spent in their kitchen during Tracy's tutorials, and he'd always been happier in her home than in his own. There had been warmth and camaraderie in the Sullivan household that had never existed at the Lander homestead.

And he felt like a traitor.

Tracy's siblings dragged him into a volleyball game and took turns spoiling Josh. His son went willingly from aunt to uncle, showing no sign of the confused, clingy baby he'd been when Cort took custody. He had Tracy to thank for that.

His gaze sought her out. She played with her niece on a quilt in the grass and talked to her sister, yet he couldn't help but notice that her smile didn't light up her eyes, whenever her gaze caught his it looked wistful.

His summer with Tracy was over, and the thought of

losing her left him aching and empty as if there'd been a death in the family.

Losing Kate had never hurt this way. But he'd loved Kate, hadn't he? Or had he just loved the way Kate made him feel competent?

From her rocking chair on Amy's back porch, Tracy cradled Josh, giving him his bedtime bottle. Laughter and the voices of her family filled the nighttime air. This was the life she'd once envisioned for herself.

Her mother settled in the rocker beside her. "Do you want to talk about it?"

She didn't know how her mother did it, but Alice Sullivan had always been in tune with her children's feelings.

Swallowing the lump in her throat, Tracy confessed, "Cort's leaving."

Her mother reached across the gap between the chairs and laid a hand on Tracy's arm. "I'm sorry."

"Me, too." A squeal from one of her nieces drew her gaze to the water gun fight in progress. Josh startled in her arms, but then went back to his bottle. The children were having a blast, and the adults were acting like children as they stalked and soaked each other. Cort was as wet as anyone.

"You could go with him."

"No. I'm needed here."

"Tracy, it would break my heart to have you living halfway across the country, but it would hurt me more to have you living nearby but miserable. We managed without your financial help before, you know, and we can do it again. Sometimes you have to do what's right for yourself."

"Staying here is what's right for me, and I don't want you going back to work. Your knees wouldn't take the strain of being on your feet all day at the diner. Besides, if Sherri passes her GED then she'll need you to look after her kids so she can go to junior college."

Her mother looked over the soggy, happy crowd in the backyard. "I'm proud of every one of my children. We didn't start with much, but you've all turned out all right."

Yes, they had, Tracy realized in surprise. She'd focused on where the Sullivan kids had gone wrong instead of where they'd gone right.

"Honey, you let him go the first time because you had to. This time you have a choice."

"Mom, I love my job, and I love the way this community rallies around to lend a helping hand to anyone in need. I don't think I'll find that anywhere else. As much as I hated the handouts, none of us would have made it as far as we have without them. It's my turn to give back."

Her mother patted her hand and rose. "Generosity is a wonderful thing, but make sure it doesn't cost you more than you have to give."

Ten

***

Cort looked up from the U-haul trailer and stopped in his tracks when all four of Tracy's brothers climbed out of their truck. He figured they'd come to beat the hell out of him for leaving their sister. He'd probably let them.

"Hey," David called out. "Tracy said you might need some help packing up."

She must have told them that he'd be coming back for her after all. "I wouldn't turn it down."

For the next hour the five of them carried boxes from the upstairs apartment until the trailer was almost full. "Thanks, guys. The only thing left is to dismantle the crib, but I'd like for Josh to finish his nap first."

David stepped forward and offered his hand. "I'm sorry it didn't work out between you and Tracy."

Tracy had told them the truth and they'd helped, anyway. The Sullivans, like Tracy, were generous even when he didn't deserve it. The knowledge humbled him. "So am I."

He loved her. The realization exploded in his head like a flashbulb and nearly brought him to his knees. How in the hell had he missed it before?

His relationship with Kate had been an attempt to replace Tracy, to find a woman who'd stand beside him and believe in him when he doubted himself. But what he'd felt for Kate had been a weak facsimile of the emotion Tracy stirred in him. He loved her, needed her and desired her.

What good would it do him to love her if he lived halfway across the country, and she wouldn't come with him? He'd have to change her mind before he and Josh pulled out of town.

As if on cue, he heard his son babbling over the baby monitor strapped to his belt. "I'd better get him."

"Cort, I would've liked having you around, but I really ought to kick your ass for hurting Tracy again."

"Again?"

"Yeah, again, and if you don't know what I'm talking about then you and my sister need to have a long talk before you hit the highway."

Was David trying to tell him that Libby's story was true? Had Tracy loved him back in high school? His heart rate doubled. Dammit, if she loved him then why not come with him?

"Hey, man, are you all right?"

"Yeah. What do you mean—"

A pickup truck—Doc's truck—came screeching around the corner interrupting his question. The vehicle skidded to a halt beside them, but Doc wasn't at the wheel. Ricardo, the fifteen-year-old who did odd jobs around the clinic was driving. "Come quick, Doc. Doc—the other one—is hurt real bad."

Adrenaline pumped through Cort's veins. Josh called on the monitor. Torn, Cort looked from the house to the truck.

David gave him a shove toward the truck. "Go, man, I'll handle Josh."

Cort hesitated. Josh had had enough upheaval in his short life. Waking up to a stranger would probably upset him.

David gave him another shove. "Go on, your little boy and I get along real well. He'll recognize his uncle David. I'll drop him off at Mom's if you don't trust the four of us."

"Let's go, let's go, let's go," Ricardo yelled from the truck.

"I'll be back as soon as I can." He passed the monitor to David. "Move over, kid. I'm driving."

The race to the clinic passed in a blur. Ricardo ranted something about Doc falling off a ladder, and then lapsed into rapid-fire Spanish. Cort couldn't understand him. Hell, it had been years since he'd used the language he used to speak almost as well as his native English.

The paramedics hadn't arrived when Cort turned into the parking lot. Pam, the receptionist, huddled over a prone form beside the building. The kite dangling from a tree branch above them and a ladder lying on its side told the tale, but Cort asked anyway—more to find out how lucid Doc was than out of curiosity.

"What happened?"

Doc's skin looked pasty and pale. "Fell off the danged ladder."

Cort did a primary survey, checking pulse, respiration

and then pulled back the blanket covering Doc and sucked in a sharp breath. "It's a bad break, Doc."

"Compound?" Doc wheezed.

Cort palpated the Doc's thigh, trying to assess the extent of the damage. "Yeah, you'll need surgical pinning. Have the paramedics been called?"

"Yes," Pam assured him. "They're on the way."

"Good. I need an inflatable splint."

"Don't have one," Doc said through gritted teeth. "Budget won't cover fancy toys."

Swearing, Cort racked his brain for something to use for a splint. If he didn't immobilize the leg, he ran the risk of having the broken bone knick the artery. He doubted the rural rescue squad had what he needed. "Ricardo, go into the clinic and take one of the shelves off the wall. Bring me the board, not the brackets, and another blanket. Pam, I need Betadine, sterile bandages, tape and anything else that will hold the board in place." Pam and Ricardo raced off.

"You're going to splint me with a bookshelf?" Doc protested.

"Give me an alternative."

"Don't have one. You always were resourceful, son, and in a low-budget practice like this, cunning is a necessary job skill." Doc grunted each word. "Ricardo's a lot like you."

And Doc had probably taken the kid under his wing the same way he had Cort fifteen years ago. "Who'll run this place while you're laid up?"

"County will send a temporary a few days a week. Don't worry about us."

"You'll be off your feet for months."

"And you'll be halfway through your cardio rotation."

He loved Tracy and if she loved him then maybe he could convince her to go back to school with him if he stayed a few more months. "Forget about a temporary. I'll stay until you're back on your feet."

"Don't pass up this rotation for me, son. If you aren't staying for yourself or for that gal, do us all a favor and go back to Duke."

"I am staying for me. Before next semester rolls around I plan to convince Tracy to go back with me."

Doc's smile looked more like a grimace. "If she convinces you to stay, I'll stand by my promise to sell you that riverfront land you've always coveted."

"Deal."

Pam brought scissors, bandages and gloves. Cort gave Doc a shot to take the edge off the pain and then cut away his pants, cleaned the open wound and packed it with gauze. With Ricardo's and Pam's help, he eased the shelf under Doc's leg. By the time the ambulance pulled into the lot twenty minutes later he'd immobilized the limb and started clearing the gear from the bed of the pickup to haul Doc to the hospital himself.

He gave the paramedics a rundown and stood back while they loaded Doc into the back. "I'll be right behind you, Doc."

The ambulance roared out of sight, and Cort's heart rate slowly returned to normal.

Ricardo stood by his side, looking up at him with hero worship in his eyes. "If you can grow up poor and still be a doc, then I can, too. Doc says so. And one day I'll come back and work here with you the way you're gonna work with Doc."

He looked into Ricardo's alert brown eyes and saw his own childhood dreams and ambitions reflected there. The preacher's words came back to him, and he realized that in the eyes of this town he'd become someone other than the youngest Lander kid. He no longer stood in his brothers' shadows.

By adopting Kate's fancy plans he'd forgotten the burning desire that had driven him through those first five years of college—the desire to give back to the folks who'd helped him. He'd allowed the promise of big bucks and a fancy office to distract him, when his entire reason for getting into medicine in the first place was to help people—*his people.*

Doctors lined up by the hundreds to make megabucks, but few signed on for the tough job of a rural physician. His community needed him here, and staying in McMullen County wasn't a sacrifice. It was a return to his original plan.

He peeled off his latex gloves and laid a hand on the teenager's shoulder. ''It takes a lot of hard work and help from your friends, but I don't doubt you'll be a doctor if you set your mind to it, Ricardo. I'll do what I can to help.''

Tracy said she only wanted him for a summer fling, but could he convince her that she needed more? He'd never failed at anything he set his heart to, but he'd never taken such a big gamble with his heart.

He grinned. It was time for Doc Lander to go a courtin'.

Tracy dropped her keys on the table and turned back to look at the trailer in her driveway. The school board had offered her the principal job and given her the weekend to make a decision.

She'd struggled for years to be in this position by taking night and weekend classes toward an advanced degree while teaching during the day. Pride and financial security had always been tremendous issues for her, so where was the elation she'd expected to feel upon attaining her goal? Why did the emptiness in the pit of her stomach threaten to swallow her?

Why wasn't she rushing to the phone to spread the news to her family and friends? Because her heart was breaking. She couldn't imagine a life without Cort and Josh, but this was where she belonged—not out there in the fancy world Cort would soon inhabit. Cort needed a wife who was his equal, and one day he'd find her.

The thought of another woman watching Josh grow up or having Cort's baby thriving inside her belly hurt. Swallowing the knot in her throat, she took a deep breath. She would get through this. Letting Cort go was the right thing to do, and if there was one thing she prided herself on it was always making the right choices. The one time she hadn't...well, look what had happened.

But before she let Cort go, she selfishly wanted to hold him one more time, to store up memories for her cold, lonely future. She headed for the inside stairs. "Cort?"

Her voice echoed back down the empty stairwell. Climbing the steps, she entered the vacant rooms, and her stomach dropped to her shoes. Other than Josh's empty crib, all Cort's belongings were gone. She sank down onto the edge of the bed they'd shared and hugged a pillow to her chest.

Where could he be? His truck was parked in front of her house with the rental trailer attached. She headed back downstairs. The blinking answering machine light called her. She punched the play button and listened to ten accounts of Doc's accident and Cort's rescue, and tears rolled down her cheeks. There was a message from her mother that David had left Josh in her care.

Swiping the moisture from her cheeks, she straightened her shoulders. Josh needed to be picked up from her mother's. And then she'd give Cort a goodbye to remember.

Tracy paced her den. An empty house had never bothered her before. In fact, after so many years of sharing a cramped bedroom with three sisters, she'd loved having a place of her own, but tonight the silence made her antsy. She actually missed tripping over Josh's toys and seeing Cort's suit coats thrown over a chair.

Her mother had refused to give Josh up, saying she'd promised Cort she'd keep him overnight. Josh certainly didn't object since her mother was spoiling him rotten, and, since she had plans of her own for Cort, she didn't argue, but she missed the little guy.

She chewed her lip and paced. She hadn't told her parents about the job offer. They'd be proud of her, but she wasn't in the mood to celebrate. They'd call her brothers and sisters, and the house would be filled to bursting. She didn't want to be with anybody but Cort and Josh tonight. They were leaving tomorrow.

Tires crunched in her driveway, pulling her back to the window for the fortieth time. Cort climbed out of Doc's truck and headed up the walk. She met him at the door. His tense, worried expression tightened a vise around her chest.

"How's Doc?"

He stopped on her doormat and didn't come inside even when she opened the door wider and stepped back. "He'll be fine. The surgery went well."

She took a deep breath. "Cort—"

"Did you get the job?"

She exhaled slowly. "Yes."

"Take a ride with me, Trace."

Her heart leaped to her throat. She'd practiced her words a dozen times already. How hard could it be to ask him to make love to her one more time for old-time's sake?

When she didn't move he shoved his hands into his pockets. "It's been one hell of a day. I'd like to watch the sun set over the river."

How could she refuse? "I'll get a sweater."

Tension filled the cab on the drive to Doc's property. Cort didn't speak, and she couldn't seem to force her request past her lips. He pulled to a stop at the end of the dirt track, backed the truck so that it blocked the road and then got out to round the cab and open her door. He offered his hand to help her out, and she couldn't seem to make herself let go of it.

"Cort, I—"

He pulled free and turned his back as soon as her feet touched the ground. Her words dried up. "I brought a blanket and dinner. Have you eaten?"

"No." She'd been too agitated to even think about food, and still was for that matter.

He carried the quilt to the riverbank, spread it out in a level spot and then returned to the truck and lifted a picnic basket from the truck bed. Tracy followed behind him and stood by, knotting her fingers and trying to find her courage while he unpacked the basket.

He set four glass-globed candles out and tossed her a pack of matches. "How about lighting those so the mosquitoes don't eat us alive? Set them on the corners of the quilt."

She did as he asked, but her fingers trembled, and

lighting the wicks wasn't as easy as it should have been. By the time she'd completed her task and the scent of citronella filled the air, he had set out plates, and a portable stereo played softly.

"You know I was planning to leave tomorrow." His somber gaze held hers as she sank down on the quilt beside him.

"Yes. About that…"

He placed a finger over her lips. "I want to make tonight a night we'll never forget."

The passion in his eyes slowly unraveled the knot in her stomach. "Me, too."

He leaned forward and touched his lips to hers in the lightest of kisses and then sat back and reached into the picnic basket.

Despite her nervousness her mouth watered. "Mmm. That smells like Mandarin shrimp."

"That's because it is." He offered her a bottle of chilled water.

"Where did you find it? It's not like we have fast food restaurants on every corner."

"Lucky for you Doc's hospitalized in San Antonio, and they do have fast food on practically every corner."

"I love Mandarin shrimp."

A smile tipped the corner of his mouth. "Your mom told me when I called to check on Josh. I have egg rolls and vegetable lo mein, too."

He reached for another container and offered her a set of chopsticks. She wrinkled her nose. "I've never been very good with those."

"Then you'll have to let me feed you. It's all in the hands, and I'm very good with my hands." His voice dropped an octave for the last line, and she nearly swallowed her tongue at the hot promise in his velvety voice.

Her body heated. "Yes, you are."

Cort tossed the paper plates back into the basket, ripped open the chopsticks, dug a large shrimp out of the carton and offered it to her. The tangy sauce exploded on her tongue, and a drop dripped on her chin. He leaned forward to sip it off, and her insides quivered. And so it went. He alternated feeding her and then himself, lapping any misplaced sauce from her chin and lips until she suspected he sometimes missed on purpose.

With one hunger sated and another aroused, she lay back on the quilt and tried to recall her speech. "No more. Cort, I—"

"Shh. Watch the sunset." He packed the leftovers back into the basket, shoved it aside and stretched out beside her. He pulled her head onto his shoulder and they watched the sun slide behind the trees. "We'll save dessert for later."

"Later?"

He rolled on his side and slid a hand beneath her shirt. His palm flattened over her belly, warming more than just her skin. "Make love with me, Trace."

"Here?" The sun had set and the moon had yet to rise. Only the dim flicker of the candles breached the darkness.

His hand stroked upward. "Nobody can see us."

Tonight would be their last night. The knowledge echoed in her head, making her question her decision to let him go. She captured his hand and pressed it to her breast, answering with actions rather than words. Could he feel her heart racing beneath his palm?

Cort shoved her sweater off her shoulders and made

quick work of the buttons on her blouse, kissing each inch of skin he uncovered. He feasted on her breasts until she squirmed beneath him on the quilt. By the time he had her shirt and bra off, her breathing was shallow. She tugged his shirt over his head and threw it aside and then kicked off her sandals.

Cort toed off his loafers, popped open the snap on her shorts and delved his tongue into her navel. Her stomach muscles clenched. The button on his jeans gave way beneath the assault of her fingers. He shucked his jeans and briefs, and she did the same until each of them lay bare on the quilt.

She'd never been naked outdoors, and she should have been inhibited, but strangely she wasn't. There was too much at stake to worry about the world around them. She rose above him, pressed his shoulders to the ground and dragged the length of her hair from his shoulders to the top of his thighs.

"Trace?" He groaned her name like a whispered plea, and she smiled against his hipbone. To date, she'd let Cort take the lead in their lovemaking, but not tonight.

Pressing a kiss against his warm skin, she caressed his torso with her hair again and again, giving the areas that made him gasp extra attention until his fists clenched in the quilt and his body trembled. She opened her lips over the thick head of his arousal in a daring move that she hadn't yet tried.

He groaned and tangled his fingers in her hair. "Trace, don't make me do this alone."

She looked at him in surprise. His eyes blazed with passion and need. "What did you have in mind?"

"We're a team. Better together than solo," he ground out.

Yes, they were, but they were a team destined to be separated.

"Jeans. Back pocket," he prompted.

She found the condom in his pants pocket, unwrapped it and rolled it over his pulsing shaft. They'd made love in many ways, but never with her on top. She straddled his thighs, easing forward until the hard length of him parted her moist folds and nudged against her focal point. She gasped as sensation erupted within her and then slid against him again and again. Waves of pleasure buffeted her.

Cort's breath whistled through his teeth. "Slow down, Trace."

"I can't."

"Then take me inside before I lose control." He caught her hips in his hands, lifted and positioned her. When she moved again he filled her, forcing all the breath from her body with the depth of his penetration. His palms skated upward to knead and pluck at her aching breasts. She moaned, lifted herself and sank again.

He arched up to meet her. She gasped and took him deeper. "Have mercy, woman."

Emotion clogged her throat. If anyone had told her a month ago that she'd be riding the man she loved on a dark riverbank, she'd have called him or her crazy.

Cort's hands shifted, and with one dexterous stroke of his finger against the swollen flesh between her legs, he sent her higher. He plied her and she rode him until the tension inside her imploded. She shuddered with pleasure, but his deep thrusts and magical touch didn't stop until pleasure swept her a second time, this time magnified by his own growling, back-bowing release.

Tracy collapsed against his chest as they both struggled to catch their breath. His arms banded around her, making her feel safe, secure and needed. She loved him. A lifetime of this didn't seem long enough, and no price seemed too high.

She couldn't let him go.

"God, I love it when you're bossy."

She heard the laughter in his voice, kissed his chin, his mouth, his nose, and then lifted herself on her arms to meet his gaze. "I want to go with you to Durham."

The amusement faded from his eyes. "No."

His flat rejection stunned, hurt and embarrassed her. She tried to scramble off his body, but he tightened his arms and she couldn't move. "You're supposed to be putting yourself first, remember? Going with me isn't what's best for you."

"That's my decision."

"No, baby, it isn't. It's our decision. We're a team, remember?"

She wanted to crawl into a hole and pull the quilt in over her, but he didn't release her. If anything his arms tightened. His lips pressed against her hair, and his chest rose and fell, lifting her as he took a deep breath.

"I'm not going back to North Carolina."

With her heart racing, she jerked upright, but he clamped his hands on her thighs, keeping their bodies joined. "You can't turn your back on your dream, Cort. I'll go with you. I'll take care of Josh."

His eyes softened, but his rejection of her offer was clear. "I called Duke and officially withdrew from the residency program today."

Her breath hitched and hope flared within her. "Why?"

"Doc's going to be off his feet for a few months. He needs me to run the clinic."

Disappointment clogged her throat. All right, so maybe it was ridiculous to hope he'd chosen to stay for her.

He tucked a stray lock of hair behind her ear. "I called the state medical board. They understand the need to rush the approval of my license and promised to have it in the next couple of days."

He sat up so that they were face to face, with her thighs still straddling his. "Fast food isn't the only thing they have in San Antonio."

Reaching into the picnic basket, he withdrew a bouquet of yellow roses and pressed the cool blooms between her breasts. The heady fragrance filled her senses. "Are yellow roses still your favorite?"

He'd bought her a single yellow bud to pin on her wrist for prom night. "Yes."

"And I'm hoping purple is still your favorite color."

This evening wasn't going at all the way she'd planned. If he didn't want her, then why was he buying her flowers? Were these pity gifts? Did he plan to stay but not to continue seeing her? "Yes."

He reached into the basket again, and her breath caught when he unclenched his fingers and offered her a blue ring box. "Open it."

She laid the flowers on the quilt beside them. Her hands trembled when she took the box and lifted the lid. Candlelight and the rising moon shone on the most beautiful deep-purple amethyst solitaire she'd ever seen. She pressed a hand to her lips and blinked at the sudden blurring of her vision. A tear trailed down her cheek.

Cort cradled her face in one warm palm. "We belong together, Trace. Marry me. Raise a family here in McMullen County with me."

She couldn't be certain through her tears, but that didn't look like convenience or pity in his eyes.

His lips brushed hers in a tender kiss. "I love you. I probably always have. And this is where I'm meant to be."

Her breath shuddered in and out, and tears rolled freely down her cheeks. He swept them away with his thumb. "But you wanted to be a surgeon."

"No, I didn't. Kate's the one who convinced me I needed a fancy office and a country club membership, but that's just not me."

"But you loved Kate."

"It took me a while to figure it out, but what drew me to Kate were her similarities to you. But she wasn't you, Trace. She didn't have your sense of community and family. She didn't have your unselfish heart, and she didn't make me feel good about being me, Cort Lander, the youngest son of a dirt-poor rancher. Kate didn't see how far I'd come. She only saw how far I still had to go before I could be the man she wanted."

His other hand joined the first, cupping her cheeks until she met his gaze. "It wasn't her voice I heard in my head when I was tired and frustrated and wanted to quit. It was yours."

"Cort, you don't have to say this. I—"

"I'm not finished here." He sipped a tear from her cheek, her chin. "It never would have worked for Kate and me because you already had my heart. She probably knew that. I realize now that I talked about you pretty often."

Her heart nearly tumbled out of her chest. She desperately wanted to believe what he said. "She gave you Josh."

"He's a great kid. For that I'll always be grateful."

"So will I, and maybe one day you can be in the delivery room for Josh's sister or brother."

His spine straightened and a light flared in his dark eyes. "Are you accepting my proposal, Miss Sullivan?"

"Yes, Dr. Lander. I most certainly am."

He sucked in a slow breath through his teeth, and his fingers slid into her hair. "Say it, Trace. I've heard it from Libby and from your brother. I need to hear you say it."

She didn't have to ask what he meant. She held his gaze, hoping he could see into her heart. "I love you, Cort. I have for a very long time, and I want to spend the rest of my life with you here, or anywhere you need to be."

"How about right here? Years ago Doc promised to sell me this land if I came back to practice in McMullen County. He's standing by that promise. Build a life and a home with me *here*, Trace, beside the river where we can come out and reenact this proposal every year on our anniversary."

"I can't think of a better place."

He banded his arms around her so tightly that she feared he'd break her ribs. "You won't regret this. That's a promise, Tracy Sullivan."

He drew back, took the ring from the box and slipped it on her finger. His lips brushed her knuckles. "I've got news for you. I'm not waiting until Christmas to marry you."

She laughed. "It's a good thing I like summer weddings."

"Then, sweetheart, we'd better call the preacher, because I'm in a hurry to get you to the altar. I can't wait to get started on our life together."

* * * * *